The Irish Barmaid   By Thomas J Monahan Sr

The Barmaid Dates Richard

Author's Note

The Grace in this story is not her real name. She was known to her friends as "The Irish Barmaid," a woman who kept a secret throughout her entire life, sharing it only with her husband. Then, only after her husband died, she shared her secret with one of her sons, asking him to keep it a secret until after she died. That son shared the secret with his wife alone until his mother died. He was then free to share the secret with the person it was about who asked him to keep it a secret from her husband and friends. The story, written as a novel, is based on some facts. The son has often wondered if he did right by sharing the secret. Sometimes people want to unlock the closet door, but by then it's both too late to turn the clock back and to re-lock the door.

I want to thank Dr. James Magee, my long-time professorial friend, for editing the manuscript.

CHAPTER 1

Callahan Is Hired out to the Neighbor.

Callahan was a tall man towering over his father by at least 5 inches. He respected his parents very much, and as their first-born son had to help with the chores around the house and sometimes take the role of a parent. Callahan had sometimes ended up caring for two brothers and three sisters younger than him, so he was the one that would come under the axe, as they say, when anything went wrong.

With so many mouths to feed and so little money, Callahan was taken out of school when his father hired him out as a laborer to a neighbor. He never saw his pay, for whatever few shillings he earned was given to his father after the harvest was sold. The work was back breaking at times, and Callahan came home drenched in sweat after working all day.

The neighbor's wife brought lunch out to the field as the Angelus bell was ringing, and they sat at the back of the cart as though they were tailgating. She removed from the satchel a few boiled potatoes and two bottles of milk. She had something special for her husband like a cut of homemade bread covered with country butter and sometimes some gooseberry jam on top. At the end of the day, Callahan was expected to remove the harness, groom and stable the horse, fill a feed bag with oats and put it on the horse's head. He was later allowed to go home.

Once at home, his mother checked his wet boots, and if she found a hole in the sole of his boot, she cutout a cardboard and slid it into the boot as an insole. The boots were hand-me-downs from his father and way too small for his big feet.

After she placed his boots next to the fire, she washed his pullover, shirt, and socks, and hung them on the crane over the fire to be dry by morning.

This was a routine for several years until one day Callahan could not take it anymore. He talked to his younger brother Brady, who had already been put on a pedestal by his father. The father regarded Brady as the smart one, and boasted to people how Brady could read newspapers and books. Callahan, on the other hand, was classed as a dummy because he could not read or write. Callahan would say, of course, that Brady was the educated one.

"I worked in the fields when Brady was sitting on his ass in a classroom getting an education. I told Brady I just could not take this kind of life anymore." Next day, Callahan told the neighbor to go find some other jerk to work for him.

The neighbor said, "You can't walk out on me in the middle of harvesting." "Yes, I can, and I will." "But I have a deal with your father." "Well, then, get my father to finish out the harvest. I quit." Callahan went home and told Brady what happened, and added, "I need to get to hell out of here. I wish I had the money to buy a ticket to America."

Brady agreed, and now that he was making some money with his horse and sidecar, he said to Callahan, "I have a little money hidden which I never told dad about. You are welcome to have it to pay for your ticket." Those two brothers were thick as thieves, and Brady was the one who told his mom and dad that Callahan was going to America. They said, "Brady, that means you will have to help around the farm here or maybe get a job. You are finished at the school, but your sisters are still going."

Callahan told his mom and dad that he would send them some money from America after he got a job. They never asked how he was going to pay for his ticket. Callahan continued, "I can't see any future here for me. I worked so hard, and no one gave a damn. I was working when other people my age were going to dances. I have never had time to ask a girl out on a date. Other people my age put their hand into their pockets and take out a fistful of change, I put my hand into my pocket and all I find is dust." The day he was leaving Brady had the horse and sidecar outside the door waiting for Callahan to leave the house. Their mother or father never came out to say goodbye.

Chapter 2

Callahan Heads for America

When Callahan finally came out and jumped up on the sidecar, Brady said, "Don't worry, Callahan. Mom and Dad will be OK. You're the first in the family to leave the country, and that's the hardest on parents. They never want to cut the apron strings on the oldest. What did Dad say?" He shook my hand and said, "Thanks for all your help," and then handed me his walking stick, the one with the silver ring on the handle.

Then he told me, "I don't want you to leave empty-handed, or, as you said before, with just dust in your pockets. Here, take this and always remember me." His mother gave him a hug and asked him to be a good lad and say his prayers every day.

Here is a strong, very tall man who can't even read or write leaving his home in County Galway and heading for America. On the way to the train, Brady looked across at Callahan, and he could see tears running down his face. Brady waited a few minutes before saying anything. "Callahan, we're all going to miss you. I can assure you mom and dad are feeling much pain that you are leaving, but they are not people that know how to express themselves." Callahan rubbed his eyes and looked at Brady as he showed him his hands palms up with the welts on them. In fact, one of them was bleeding where Callahan had scratched it.

Brady added, "Callahan, you will do fine in America. I was reading in one of those foreign newspapers how some companies are looking forward to hiring able bodied immigrant men because they are the best workers and are willing to work long hours. They make very good money, most of which they sent back to help their families at home. You should have no problem getting a job."

After arriving at the train station, Brady tied the horse to a pole and walked with Callahan up to the platform where he shook his hand and said goodbye. His last word to Brady was, "Take care of mom and dad." Brady answered, "Callahan, please get someone to write me a letter, and tell me how you are getting on in America."

Callahan's parents were not too happy that he was leaving, but they knew they could not stop him. The train ride was new to him, and then at the docks he saw this big boat tied with thick ropes to iron rings on the dock. There were two lines of people waiting to get on board, both moving very slowly while a tall man dressed in a blue uniform was checking the papers. As Callahan got closer, he could see two wide planks of wood used as a walkway to the boat.

Most people had suitcases. Some had burlap bags over their shoulder. When Callahan handed his papers to the man in uniform, the man asked him where his luggage was. "The only luggage I have is the clothes on my back and this walking stick which belongs to my father." The man directed him to follow the crowd. After walking up the planks, he entered an opening in the side of the boat and found there were people everywhere climbing up three more flights of stairs.

At the top of the stairs he met another man in a blue uniform who asked to see his papers, and told him he was going in the wrong direction. Callahan flushed, "What do you mean I'm going in the wrong direction? I'm following the people just as the man below told me to do." The man replied, "According to your papers, you need to head down five flights of stairs to steerage." Callahan argued, "Why can't I follow those people in front?" The official said, "Don't you see they are in suits. They are passengers heading to first class. You are going to steerage."

Callahan headed to the steerage section five flights down where he met a man in uniform who wanted to see his papers. Callahan asked, "What's with the papers that you are all looking at? The officer explained, "The papers tell us where you are going, what deck you are assigned to, and what bunk you are going to spend the next twelve to fourteen days in. Sir, please follow me. Sir, here is your room."

When Callahan entered the room, he hit his head on the top of the door opening and cursed. "This is a hole in the wall, and they call it a room! There is a tiny bed only fit for a child, and I am a big strapping man." He put the walking stick in the corner up against a small chest of drawers which he left empty since he had nothing to put into them. He went up several flights of stairs to the upper deck where he looked out over the water. "Am I crazy heading out into this big ocean? What if this boat sinks? I can swim a little but no way in hell could I swim to shore." He walked to the railing and looked down at the water. The deck he was on was much higher than the water.

Callahan determined to enjoy the next twelve to fourteen days they said it will take to get to America. He looked back at the dock and his last glimpse of Ireland for a while. There he heard someone say,   "Hello, you must be heading for America." Callahan turned around and looked at this man in the face, , "Where in the hell do you think I'm heading? Of course, I'm heading for America, and where are you heading?"

"Oh, I'm heading for America too. This is a big boat, a lot bigger than the one I had at home. I gave mine to my brother when I left because he likes to fish. By the way, my name is Porter and

what is yours? And what county are you from?"
"I'm Callahan, and I'm from County Galway. How
about you?" "I'm from Galway too, little village
called Glenn." "Sure, I know it well. I'm from the
next village called Templemore."

Porter continued, "This boat is getting a little
wobbly. Let's hold on to the rail, or we might fall
overboard. Tell me, Callahan, why are you going
to America?" "Well, Porter, it's like this. I got sick
and tired of working my ass off for very little
money in return." "That's funny, Callahan, I did
the very same thing. Do you have any friends in
America?" "I have a few relatives somewhere
over, but I have no clue as to where they are. They
never write, and I heard my mother say one time
they are cheap bastards. One time she wrote to
them that she received their letter, and it was
empty, meaning there was no money in it. She
thinks that's why they stopped writing. If they
send a letter, they think they would have to put

some dollars into it. Porter, I do have a cousin in New York in a place called Brooklyn, and my mother said she heard he has a great job. From what she was told, he ran New York City. He worked for a big-name company called sanitation dept. One time she said he wrote and said he was head of the prison system, but later she found out he was a prisoner there, the lying bastard. Maybe I will meet up with him when this boat docks in New York."

After chatting for some time they discovered that Porter's mother was a first cousin to Callahan's neighbor. Porter asked Callahan why he kept rubbing his head. "I hit in on the door opening to what they called a room." Porter replied, "I don't have to worry about hitting my head, because I'm a short little guy. They used to call me the smartest little guy when I was going to school."

The ship sailed from Belfast and docked thirteen days later at the port of New York. The day before they arrived in New York, Porter introduced Callahan to a man he met in the bar on one of the upper decks. His name was Duff Murphy, and he was heading to Pittsburgh to work in the mines. Duff said he had a brother who was already working in the mines and had some "pull," as they say. Callahan and Porter asked Duff if it was OK for them to travel with him to Pittsburgh in the hope that they might get work there. Porter said, "You could tell your brother that you knew us very well, or you might even say we are related. Otherwise, we might have to pay a visit to Brooklyn and look up my cousin there. Duff replied, "I'll do my best for you guys. Let's all go to Pittsburgh and see if we can get a job." Callahan tapped Porter on the shoulder and said, "If we get a job, will you do me a favor and write a letter to my brother Brady? I'll give you a few

18

dollars to put into it for my mother, so she doesn't
tell the neighbors that her son is a cheap bastard."

Chapter 3

Callahan Arrives in Pittsburg

Callahan, Duff, and Porter arrived in Pittsburgh
the next morning. After they asked a few people for
directions to the mines, they got a bus part way and
then started to walk. A huge truck stopped and the
driver shouted, "You know people walking three
abreast like you guys could cause an accident;
would you guys like a ride?" Porter answered, "Yes,
thank you, sir. You are most kind." They could tell
by the size of the truck and dirty face of the driver
that it had to be from the mines. The driver asked
where they came from and Porter said, "We just
came over from Ireland." "I know that from your
clothes and your brogue, but what county in Ireland
are you from?" Porter replied jokingly, "I'm from
the only county in Ireland and that's county

Galway." The driver laughed and asked if he knew a place called Glenn? Porter exclaimed, "Holy Crap! I'm from Glenn." The driver continued, "I came over from there six years ago. My name is Charles Foley." Porter repeated the name, "Would you be a son of Marie Foley from the cross roads?" "Aye, So you must know my mother then? Does she still laugh as loud as ever? She was always one to tell a joke and then laugh at it herself. Tell me, Porter, how is my mother doing these days?" Porter said, "I'm sorry to have to tell you this, but she died last year. I heard someone at the burial say they could not contact her son because he never wrote since he left home."

Charley stopped the truck, and got out because he felt sick. He went to the side of the road, sat down, and cried. Then stood up and shouted as loud as he could, hoping his mother could hear him, "Mother, I am so sorry. I should have never left home. Please forgive me." Porter walked over and putting his hand on Charles shoulder said, "Come now, Charley, I can tell you she did not suffer. She died suddenly from a heart attack." Charley shook his head, "No, she died from a broken heart. She never wanted me to leave home. I never wrote to her because I don't know how to write, and I was too embarrassed to ask someone to write a letter for me." Callahan said, "That will never happen to me. I will find someone to write a letter to my brother Brady and tell him where I am. You see, Charlie, I can't read or write either. But Porter here can do both since he went to school."

With all four in the truck including Charley behind the wheel, Duff asked Charlie if he ever heard of a Redmond Murphy? Charley replied, "Sure, everyone knows Redmond. He works in coal mine Number one. I will drop you off there. We have several mines and hundreds of people working here." They all thanked Charley for the ride, and walked to the hut that had a sign over the door

which read "supervisor". Duff introduced himself as
Duff Murphy, the brother of Redmond Murphy, and
asked the man with all the papers and note books if
Redmond worked here. It seemed Redmond was
well-known and liked by all. The supervisor stood
up from his chair and shouted. Redmond, please
come here? I have a surprise for you. Redmond
shouted, "Don't tell me someone is trying to pass
themselves off as a cousin of mine again. No,
Redmond, this time, he's claiming he is your
brother."

"For God's sake, get rid of him. Sure, the only
brother I have is back in County Galway."
"Redmond, I think you had better come here and
take a look at this fellow. From the looks of him, he
could pass as your twin." Redmond stuck his head
out the door of the shed and shouted, "Holy crap, it
is my brother, and he is my twin." After they shook
hands and danced around a little. Duff asked
Redmond if he would give a job to his friends

Callahan and Porter. Duff answered, "Bring him along. Sure, if he is a friend of yours, he must be a good worker." All three went into the canteen and sat chatting for the next few hours.

Duff asked Redmond, "Why is it you only wrote one letter home in all those years?" "Well, brother, let me tell you I was too busy, what with getting married and now having a spouse and two sons to care for. Where do you think I would get the time to write home. On top of that, did dad ever tell you he took me out of school to work on the damn farm? So you see I am no good at writing or spelling for that matter." "Tell me, Redmond, is your wife Irish?" "Duff, you will meet her on the weekend and bring Callahan along with you. I'm sure you both could use a good home-cooked meal of spaghetti and meatballs. Redmond looked at Callahan, "She can't be Irish. She must be Italian."

"You guys just met the supervisor. Well, he is my father-in-law. That's why I can take some time to sit and chat with you guys. Let me show you to your bunks, and then I will get you some food and work clothes. Now, lads, the work is hard, and we don't do well with anyone who tries to goof off. There are no warnings here; you just get fired. Try your best to stay out of other people's fights. I have to run now, or I might get fired myself. There is no mercy here. You work in the mines digging for coal from morning until night and sometimes there is not enough water to wash the dust from your face. You might wear the same clothes day in and day out without washing them. I will meet you in the food tent later, and don't forget you start work tomorrow morning at 7:00 A.M. Duff, please keep it under your hat that you're my brother or people might think I'm into favoritism. You will come into my house over the weekend and meet my wife and sons. Lads, let me tell you working at the mines is not easy. The work is hard and the dust is a killer, but the money is good."

Callahan was saving his money since he wanted to return to Ireland and start some kind of business other than farming. His goal was to make and save as much money as he could while he was in America. He was not afraid of hard work as long as it was not farming. Porter and Callahan became the best of buddies, and watched out for each other. Porter made timekeeper after a short time because he went to school. You see, his father did not take him out of school to work on the farm. Callahan, on the other hand, could not read or write so he was stuck with digging and would always be a laborer doing the heavy work.

For the next few years, Callahan and Porter worked at the mines. It was back breaking work, but, as they always said, the money was good. Callahan was only sick twice in those two years, once when he cut his leg on a drill after the supports gave way and the ceiling tumbled down. He could not work for a few weeks. Another time he got the measles and was quarantined for a short time. The workers would say that Callahan was the strongest man in the team,

One-day Porter asked Callahan if he was OK. "You look like you are losing weight. Are you eating all of the crapy food they give you here?" Callahan said, "I feel fine. Don't be like an Irish mother always asking, 'Did you eat enough?'" One morning, though, Callahan did not show up for work and Porter went to see why. When he found Callahan lying in his bunk with blood on the pillow, Porter took him to see the doctor. He was diagnosed with black lung disease. The doctor had no choice but to give the report to the boss, and that was the end of Callahan working at the mines. He was let go. Porter took the rest of the day off to spend with Callahan, and arranged to have all of Callahan's monies, including any back pay which came to a lot of money, given to Callahan.

The foreman gave the OK for Callahan to stay around for a few weeks or so, and use the bunk and get some free meals because of Duff's brother. Callahan bounced back but his breathing was not as good as when he first started working in the mines. As time went on Callahan felt much better and he tried talking to some of the bosses in hopes of getting his job back. They said they would consider it based on the doctor's report. Callahan did all the right things. He stopped drinking and ate good food before checking in with the doctor for a checkup. The doctor checked Callahan's lungs, but found that his breathing remained compromised. So, the doctor's report was not helpful. There was no future for Callahan in Pittsburgh.

Chapter 4

Callahan Returns to Ireland

Callahan decided to head back home to Ireland. He
had more clothes now than when he arrived, and
packed them into a pillow case. He took his father's
walking stick, said good-bye to all his friends, and
headed for the train which would take him to New
York City. He had quite a bit of money which he
stuffed into his extra boots and then wrapped with
some other clothes before putting them into the
pillow case. His friends Porter and Redmond
Murphy drove him to the train.

He set sail on the next ship back to Ireland. He had
had Porter write a letter for him to his brother
Brady, and asked that Brady meet with him at the
train station in Galway on such and such a day. Sure

enough Brady was there waiting for Callahan, whose first words were, "How are mom and dad?" Brady looked into Callahan's face with tears in his eyes, and said they both passed away last year six months apart. "The damn tuberculosis, sure it has killed so many people in those last two years. Mom and dad kept saying to people they met, 'We hope Callahan is ok.' They did miss you, but I took care of them. Rest assured, they did not go hungry, and the sisters finished school." Brady stopped at the next pub, and put the feed bag on the horse's head. They went in and had a pint of Guinness. Callahan told Brady about his illness and that he felt fine right now. He said in joking that the doctors told him he could have a short life. "But what do they know. We Irish are strong; we always hope to outlive our parents." As they finished the pint of Guinness, Brady remarked, "I see you still have the dad's walking stick." "Yes, indeed, and it saved my life one time. I was jumped by a few lads, and I can tell you I would not want to have their heads the next morning. Perhaps we had better leave now; it's a long drive home." Brady took the feed bag from the horse's head and placed it in the sidecar, and they headed home. As they arrived in the next village, they stopped and went into Molloy's pub for another pint.

It was daylight now and Callahan, pointing to some people working in the fields and others working in the bogs, remarked, "Now that's back breaking work. That's why I left Ireland to begin with. The work is fine, but the pay is poor." Callahan also spotted three girls picking potatoes in a field. Brady identified them as the Clancy Girls. "None of them ever married. I think Clancy keeps the men away from the door because he does not want to lose good cheap help."

After Callahan had rested up from a few days at home, he asked Brady to drive him down around Clancy's house, so he could get a good look at those girls. Brady stopped the horse at the end of the road leading to the field, and Callahan looked at one girl in particular. She wore a long black apron, and her sister wore a red apron. Callahan smiled at Brady and asked him if he would take him to the matchmaker in the area so he could talk to him. Brady answered, "We only have two matchmakers in the area now that Cunningham with the limp died a few years ago. He was one that could make a good deal for the dowry. Right now the best one I hear is Sweeney from Cloone." "That's fine with me, Brady. Maybe you will you take me to him tomorrow." "It will have to be early morning since I have to drive some people to the afternoon train. In fact, it's a family of three and they are heading for America. They were evicted, lost their house to the landlord, and their son sent them the money from America for their passage. He has a spread of a few hundred acres in Oklahoma."

Chapter 5

Callahan Meets with the Matchmaker

The next day they met Sweeney the matchmaker who warned Callahan, "I can tell you now Clancy is a hard egg to crack. Would you consider paying a visit to Carter the weaver has a few daughters and lots of land? Callahan replied, "Mr. Sweeney, I want to go meet Clancy." Sweeney plotted, "I will ride with you to the Clancy house, and go in first to soften him up. This way he will be nice to you." A short time later Sweeney beckoned Callahan to come in and meet Clancy who was sitting at the table having a cup of tea while Mrs. Clancy was pounding away at the churn in the middle of the floor.

Sweeney introduced Callahan to Mr. and Mrs. Clancy who invited him to join them for tea. The matchmaker told the Clancy's why there were there, that Callahan was home from America and would like to marry one of the girls. You did not insult a matchmaker since he might never come again, and you might have three daughters on your hands for the rest of your life. Mr. Clancy asked his three daughters to come to the kitchen and sit on a wooden bench by the window. This way Callahan could get a good look at all three. "Which one of my girls did you want to marry?" "Now hold on a minute," said the matchmaker. "Not so fast. Let the man look them over first, and then him and I will have a talk in private." After the private chat, Callahan decided to pick the girl on the right end of the bench, the one who she wore the red apron. She looked like the oldest.

"Well, Mr. and Mrs. Clancy, I think Callahan has decided. Now let's get to the dowry. What will

you be giving your daughter on her wedding day?
Callahan here and I will decide what you will get in
return for your daughter? It was decided that the
daughter would get one heifer and two sheep and in
return, the Clancy's would get three gold
sovereigns. The exchange would happen the
afternoon of the wedding. Then the girls were sent
back out to the fields. Callahan shook hands with
Mr. and Mrs. Clancy, and said goodbye.

A few weeks went by, and Callahan asked
Brady if he and his new bride could live with Brady
until he could buy a place of his own. Brady said it
was ok with him, and smiled, "I might get a home
cooked meal from time to time. You know,
Callahan, I'm a hard one to please. That's why I
have not married. Maybe I should have Sweeney
take me to see Carter the weaver. I could end up
with a few acres of land." Callahan fixed up
Brady's house for the newlyweds, but he knew it

would be only temporary. Callahan wanted a house
of his own.

Chapter 6

Callahan Gets Married

On the day he was getting married Callahan
arrived outside the church all spruced up. He was
driven there by his brother Brady with his horse and
sidecar. Brady must have worked all night preparing
the horse and sidecar. The harness of the horse was
all polished, and the brass hames had a glitter to it.
Brady even had the horse's hoofs polished with
black shoe polish. Callahan arrived way ahead of
the bride to be. Keep in mind Callahan had only
seen his future spouse twice, first in the field
picking potatoes second, on the day he went with
the matchmaker to her house. Clancy arrived
outside the church in his pony and trap with the new
bride all dressed up. I would say that Clancy's wife
spent most of the night cleaning and polishing the
trap. Clancy was one of those people that would

step over the broom that fell down across the entrance into the house and wait for someone to come behind him to pick it up. Callahan was waiting for the priest at the Alter. Mr. and Mrs. Clancy entered the church with their three daughters. Mrs. Clancy and two of the daughters went to a seat up front. The bride-to-be walked to the altar by her father's side. Then he handed her over to Callahan with a handshake. Callahan looked surprised as he smiled at the new bride to be. He took a double take. He looked again at the bride to be but said nothing for the moment. However, he knew something was wrong he looked again at the bride to be and thought to himself, "This is not the girl I picked to be my wife." He turned his head and whispered something in the ear of the priest. The priest excused himself from the crowd and asked Callahan to follow him into the sacristy. When there the priest asked Callahan if he wanted to go ahead with the wedding, Callaghan said, "I think so."

"Even after what you whispered into my ear."

Callahan said, "She is so beautiful, but she looks so young. The priest said, "Let's put it in God's hands." They returned to a stunned crowd who was wondering what was happening. Callahan stood up straight, shoulders back, and smiling as he looked at this beautiful bride standing there and smiling back at Callahan. Then wedding took place.

A few years later, Callahan found out what really happened. Clancy had only three daughters and no sons. So, he had to get the two youngest daughters married off before his oldest daughter could marry and have her husband move to the house. The custom was that the first-born son got the house and in this case, the firstborn daughter got the house. Clancy never went to America, but he knew what he was doing. After the wedding, everyone went to Callahan's house for food and drink. They had a sing-song, and everyone got to know each other. A few hours went by and there was a knock at the door it was the matchmaker dressed in his black coat and top hat. They welcomed him in. He raised his glass to toast the newlyweds, and then he said, "Time to go outside and meet my brother Tom." He was holding on to a few halters, one attached to a heifer and one attached to two sheep. The matchmaker announced that it was time to exchange the dowry. He handed the halters to Callahan, and Callahan handed him the three sovereigns which the matchmaker handed to Clancy. The Matchmaker said, "The deal is now closed and may the newlyweds have many sons and daughters. Now let's fill up the glasses and let the party continue."

The party went on into the night with music from someone with an accordion, and another person had a Jew's harp. Callahan gave a speech, he started by thanking Mr. and Mrs. Clancy for letting him marry their daughter. Then he thanked the matchmaker. And thanked all the friends and foe who are here to celebrate their wedding. He then went over to his wife and kneeled in front of her and said, "Alannah we are going to be the envy of the village. We will have sons and daughters like no one has ever seen. We will take care of each other until death does us part." He then gave her a big kiss this was their first kiss ever.

The crowd shouted and screamed and the pot-walloping with Callahan's walking stick in the empty pot and bucket by the fire. The party ended the next morning. The Clancy's headed for home in their pony and trap. Callahan and His new spouse Alannah walked the fields chatted and exchanged stories. They even held hands as they strolled through the fields. They found out that Callahan was years older than Alannah.

That did not matter now that they were newly wedded, and they were going to have the best of a marriage newlywed couple did not plan on when they were going to have children. It just happened. Then Callahan said, "Alanna, we need to have our own home. We don't want to be living in Brady's house during the rest of our life." You see Brady inherited the house after his parents died in as much as Callahan had left home. Callahan went to work for the same neighbor he worked for before going to America. Callahan knew it was only temporary. He bought a horse and saddle. Indeed, he was a great rider, and told Brady, "All I need now is a gun and holster and I could be a cowboy." He asked Brady if he could use an old shed next to his father's house for a short time as a forge. Brady answered, "Of course you can use it. Sure, if you had not gone to America, you would own it."

Callahan had learned a lot from his travels. He started by putting shoes on horses and repairing carts. One day a neighbor stopped he had a loose rim on the cartwheel and asked if he could do something with it. He removed the wheel and the rim and started up his fire with charcoal which he had previously burned. He heated the rim and placed it on the wheel and then cooled it instantly with cold water so it had shrunk to the size of the wheel. Word spread fast about this blacksmith who was home from America, and customers came daily to have their horses shod and shovels welded. He made a little money, not a lot. He and Alannah were very happy. One day a man from the next village came to his forge and asked Callahan to replace all the shoes on his horse. The horse had thrown a shoe and was limping a bit. Callahan lifted the front leg of the horse and found a small stone stuck in the frog of the hoof. He removed the stone and doused the leg with poteen as a cure all.

This man knew just about everyone in the area, even where they pissed last. He said, "Callahan, I heard you were in America and how was it there? Oh, by the way my name is Jim. I come from the next village, a place called Templemore. I hear America is a big country, and no one talks to anyone over there because they are too damn busy

making money. He said years ago I was thinking of
going there. I had my ticket and all got, but then I
met this woman and we got married. That was the
end of my travel. I gave the ticket to my cousin
Porter. Funny how he never wrote to us; I have no
idea where he ended up. I hope he did not take to
the drink and end up in that place called the
Bowery. I hear there are a lot of people there."
Callahan responded, "I'm sure he's all right
otherwise you would have heard." Callahan never
told him he knew or worked with Porter. Callahan
was not one to give out information about his time
in America since he did not want people to know he
was sent home because of the black lung disease.
He felt the fewer people knew about him the better.
The man said, "Callahan" I hear there is a pub not
too far away, and it might be going into the market
for sale soon. I hear the owner has a little trouble
paying her bills it might be worth looking
into. Next day Callahan paid a visit to the pub and
asked for a Guinness. The owner, a woman who

could talk the fur off a cat, said her husband had died a few years ago, they had no kids, and now her money was running out, so she was thinking of selling the place. "Callahan, how was it in America? I wish I had gone before I married my husband. Sure, he could drink the Shannon River dry and whatever profit we made here as well. Would you know anyone that would be interested in buying a pub? I don't live here I have my own house over the road?" Callahan asked, "How much would you be looking for it, if I might ask?" She answered, "I figured out all the bills I owe and what it cost us to buy it some years ago, and I subtracted what I think it would cost to make some repairs. I would need to get so and so pounds." Callahan said he would keep his ears open and let her know.

Alanna was very good in school, could read and write, and was good at sums. So, Callahan brought the opportunity up to Alannah, "I think I will make her an offer tomorrow. This way we can have our

own place and a business, as well."- Alanna
answered, "Callahan, you know best." Next day
Callahan stopped into the pub for a pint of
Guinness, chatted with the owner, and made her an
offer. She accepted his offer and said he could move
in right away. "This way I'll be adding years to my
life since it was killing me with worry about being
able to pay my bills." Callahan had someone draw
up a contract and read it to him. He put an X on the
paper as his signature, and the deal was set.
Callahan had enough money saved from his time in
America that he could pay her in cash. This way,
she could pay off her bills and retire. Brady and
Callahan moved whatever few items he had into the
pub, and Callahan fixed it up nicely. Alanna was
ever so happy. The first day he opened the pub for
business, there was a line outside the door with
pony and traps lined up. Outside you could hear
people say, "The pub has a new owner, a yank,
mind you, a big shot who was in America for a
while, and today the drinks are for free!"

Chapter 7

The Irish Barmaid Is Born

Callahan and Alannah were so happy that they would sit and talk for hours. He would run his fingers through her long jet black hair, look into her eyes, and say, "You are beautiful, and yet you look different from other girls." She smiled, "That's because I am told I have some Spanish blood in my veins. They say when the Spanish Armada ships sank along the West coast of Ireland some of the survivors intermarried with the Irish, and I must be related to one of them." "That's why your face looks different. I love it and I love you and I hope out children look like you.

In this best of times Alannah had her first baby whom they named Grace. Callahan was happy that his pub was doing a good business, and would say to Alannah, "I am doing very well for someone who can't read or write, but you are my backbone, and I am so happy you are the one that your father and mother picked to send to the church on that special day. He would look at Grace, and say in a few years she will be working for me as a barmaid. Several other children were born to them, but Grace remained special since she was their first born. Grace went to school and was really smart. As she got older, she did all the bookwork for her dad. She ordered the supplies and was one of the best barmaids.

Everyone loved her. She had her mother's smile, and her father would say that she is growing up so fast she is a woman now. She even has a boyfriend. One day, Grace was missing, and Callahan asked Alannah where she had gone. Alanna began to worry because it was not like Grace to leave the bar unattended with people helping themselves by filling their pints of Guinness and leaving the money on the counter. Alanna pleaded that Callahan should go down by the water to see how she was. By the water he found Grace sitting upon a rock with her feet below the water. Callahan sat next to her, put his hand over her shoulder, and asked if she was all right. Tears were running down her face. "Dear child," said Callahan, "what is wrong?" "Daddy, I'm pregnant, and I don't know what to do. Are you going to send me away to the nuns' house?" "Come, my child, let's go tell your mother. She will know what to do." Callahan and Grace walked back to the pub and into the kitchen where Alanna was sitting and worried but so happy to see Grace was all right. Callahan said, "I will leave you two alone. Grace here has something she wants to tell you." Well, Alannah and Grace talked for some time, and finally Grace went behind the bar, started serving drinks as best she could, and collected the money which was left on the counter by the customers who had filled their own drinks.

Callahan was happy to see Grace behind the counter, and went to the kitchen to talk to Alannah. Alanna was crying, and told him, "Grace said she was pregnant and is afraid we will send her away to the nuns and disown her from the family." Callahan sat next to her. "This is a big decision we have to make together. Tell me, Alannah, what's in your mind? Sure, she is a good girl, and we can't throw her out. What do you say we should do?" "Callahan, I have been so happy with you even though we were not in love when we married. We are now, and she is part of us. So I think we should let her have the child, and we will raise it as best we can. Otherwise Grace's life will be destroyed." "Alanna, you are a wise woman. When will the baby be born?" "It will be a few months from now." "Ok, that's settled then. I guess we are going to have ourselves another child. Hope that God gives us good health, and helps us on the way."

Grace gave birth to a beautiful baby girl. The father at first denied being the father, but one day, he approached Callahan and Alannah and asked to talk to them. He said there was not much future here to support a child, so he planned to go to America. After he was settled down and with a little money in his pocket, he would send for Grace and the baby. It sounded good as he was telling it. Callahan remembered when he thought the same way, that there was no future around here and no money, so he gave it some thought. Days later, the father arrived again and asked Callahan if he would sign his name to a paper that the police department gave him. When he had applied for a passport, he was told that they had heard he had fathered a child and, therefore, would have to have the girl's father sign the form giving permission for the father to leave the country before they could issue a passport. Callahan talked it over with Alannah, and both trusted his word and thought it would be good for everyone concerned. This way Grace and the baby could travel to America at a later date. Callahan put his signature, an X, on the form, and the father sailed to America. Weeks went by, then months, then years, and the bastard never wrote. Even his family had no idea where he went or where he ended up.

Grace was still the Barmaid, always with a smile on her face while her mother raised the child as Grace's sister. Grace was now a young woman, and felt that she had destroyed her life. Her self-esteem was as low as it could go. Sometimes she wished she could turn the clock back, and have listened to her mother who would always tell her daughters to open your legs only to Pee. To think that she loved the bastard! Sometimes she would say under her breath, "I hope he rots in hell!"

Chapter 8

Gossip Inside Callahan's Pub

The Barmaid had now completed her growth, a tall 5 Feet, 10 inches. She stood behind the counter, her eyes shining with dark hair and a radiant smile. Around her waist, she wore a green and red plaid apron. As some patrons entered the bar, she greeted them by their first names. Most were regulars and came there to have a drink and shoot the bull, as they say. When four of her friends, Liam, Peter, Willie, and Shamus entered, she said, "Hello boys, should I draw you the usual?" The usual was three pints of Guinness and one medium which is less than a pint. She could tell who the designated driver was since he would be the one drinking the medium. All four were neighbors from the next village and were picked up by Liam in his pony and trap. Liam, Peter, and Willie sat down at the table in the corner.

Shamus walked to the counter and asked the Barmaid for an extra chair. She handed him a low three-legged stool which she took from inside the counter. He went back to the table and handed the stool to Liam who was the tallest of the four. From time to time, they would look around at the patrons in the bar, and comment about others who were there having a drink. Liam, "Lads! Don't look right now, but I see George over there by himself; he and the wife must be fighting again. That's the fourth shot of whiskey he has downed one after the other." Willie, "You think I should go over and talk with him?" "Liam, Willie, stay where you are. Don't you remember last month when Billy Joe tried to talk to him? Sure, he slugged him one in the face and broke his nose, and no one has seen Billy Joe since? Peter, "Well, lads, he is now drinking Guinness. Hope he doesn't fall from his bicycle on the way home." Liam, "What are you looking at, Peter? I'm looking at the Barmaid; she is such a beautiful girl. What a beautiful smile she has. I can't imagine her having a child almost five years old, and she not even married. I heard the father took off to America after the priest went to see him and told him he would have to marry the girl. He was never seen since. He must be a real bastard." Willie, "Are you sure he is the father, Liam ? Sure he is. I heard it from the housekeeper who works in the rectory for the priests. I'm sure she heard it first-hand." Peter, "I heard he was blaming Sonny, you know, Katie's son from the hill beyond."

Liam, "Sonny wouldn't harm anyone. Sure Sonny's mother would never let him have a girlfriend. Shamus, "I understand that her mother is raising the kid for her. The kid must be five or six years old by now. It's nice that Callahan gave her a job here in his bar. I'm surprised she never went to work in England."Liam, "I understand her mother is a very nice woman." Seamus, "Most mothers and fathers would have beaten her and throw her out of the house and she would not be allowed to return since she had disgraced the family name." Willie, "Or worse still, place her into a mother's baby home run by them nuns." Willie, "Thank God the mother is caring for the baby. Sure, I hear some of those homes are terrible. I hear they abuse the poor girls and make them work like slaves, and sometimes they sell the babies to foreigners for a lot of money."

Chapter 9

A Stranger Enters Callahan's Pub

The door opened, and a well-dressed not so tall man entered and walked up to the bar. Liam, "Shush, guys! Let's hear who the stranger is and where he comes from." "Peter, "Can you hear him from there?"Liam: "Yes, he asked for a pint of Guinness. He just took a pack of cigarettes from his pocket. Let's see if he shares them around. He must be a cheap bastard; he put the pack of cigarettes back into his pocket." Peter went over and stood next to him, but he moved away and went to the end of the counter where the paraffin single wick lamp was burning. With the cigarette in his mouth, he put the end over the glass globe and lit the cigarette.

The stranger returned to his pint on the counter, and side-stepped around Peter, who was standing there. Peter said, "Hello! You're a stranger here and where do you come from?" He nodded, "Yes, I am. Why would think otherwise?" Peter answered, "The Irish always share the cigarettes with the people sitting or standing next to them." "Oh, he said, do you want a cigarette? I have some" He took the pack from his pocket, pulled one cigarette out a little from the pack, and pointed the pack towards Peter. Peter reached out his hand and took the whole pack, removed the cigarette, and walked over to his friends and passed the cigarettes around. Peter whispered to Liam, "I'll strike up a conversation with him and invite him over here for a chat. He might buy us all a drink."

It turned out he was a very nice fellow. He told us he came like the three wise men from the East, meaning east of where they were right now. We chatted a bit, and he said that he had rented a small shop not too far from here.

Liam, "And what is your name, if I might ask?" Stranger, "Oh, my name is it? If you want to know, they call me 'Richie'. Most people call me 'Richard'." Liam, "And what do you sell in the shop you rented, and who did you rent it from?" Richard, "Oh, you want to know what I sell and who I rented the shop from?"

Liam, "Yes, we would like to know. We might know the person you rented from."

Peter, "Stop, Liam, you are confusing Richard here with all your questions. Sure, maybe he is undercover for the IRA."

Liam, "Peter, you worry too much. Sure, Richard here does not at all look like an IRA man."

Willie, "Well now, lads, I have been sitting here and listening to you all shoot the bull. Will you just ask the man to tell you his life's history and stop beating around the bush."

Richard: Well said. First of all, I am not an IRA man, so you can all settle down and be quiet. I am a butcher, and I rented the shop from Charlie Dempsey."

Liam, "Sure, we all know Charlie. He has the finest flock of sheep this side of the Shannon River. His wife, God rest her soul, just died a few months ago, and if she were alive right now, she would not let Charlie rent anything. She was a tough woman. She was a Murphy from Cregg. Her father was a blacksmith and a very good one at that. Let me also tell you he is one of the biggest crooks around. You better count your money twice before handing it to him."

Richard, "Can I buy you all a round of drinks?"   Liam, "We thought you would never ask. Sure, I'll have a full pint this time; the pony knows his own way home.

Peter, "I'll go tell Grace to bring us a round of drinks."

Grace arrived over with the drinks on a tray and placed the drinks on the table.

 Liam, "Richard I want you to meet Grace. She is the owner's daughter."

Richard, "Hello Grace! Are those men giving you a hard time?"

Grace, "Not at all. Sure, they are happy-go-lucky lads just here to enjoy a drink and chat with the neighbors. I'm sure they have asked you a lot of questions. If I were you, I would not tell them too much. Sure, it will be all over the country by tomorrow."

Peter, "Come now, Grace, we are not that bad. Sure, Grace, if you are nice to Richard here, he might ask you out."

Grace, her face getting red, said, "Peter, that's enough talk out of you. Sure, you have been asking me for a date for months now."

Liam, "OK, let us all be quiet now so Richard can pay Grace for the drinks." Grace, "Nice meeting you, Richard! I hope to see you again. Don't be a stranger."

Liam, "I think Grace has the eye for Richard here, but, sure, Richard would not be interested in Grace. She has a child out of wedlock."   Peter
, "Stop that kind of talk now, Liam. Grace is a very nice girl. Sure, it's the child's father I blame, and the bastard taking off to America and leaving her and the baby behind."

Seamus, "Enough of that gossip now; I have to be going home. Are your guys ready?"

Liam, "For Christ's sake, will you give me time to down my drink, will you?

Richard, "Well, nice meeting you all maybe we will meet again sometime." Richard said good night to Grace and said he hoped to see her another time.

Chapter 10

The Barmaid Refuses a Date

A few days later, Richard arrived at the pub on his bicycle. This time he was the only one in the pub besides Grace, and they struck a little chit-chat, with him asking her where he could buy some poteen. She answered that she did not think anyone made it anymore around here. The guards were always on the watch, and people were afraid because there were a lot of weasels around. He told her a little about himself and asked her if she would like to go out on a date with him. Her face went red, and she complained, "You got some nerve asking me out on a date, and neither one of us knows anything about each other." He replied, "What there is to know, sure, that would come as we date."

She persisted, "I will consider it if you tell me a little more about yourself, and I will tell you a little about me." He said, "That's fine. Let's start with me. I am single and have never been married." He added jokingly, "I have no kids." That seemed to put the kibosh on things. She went to the back room as if to get some supplies, wiped her face on her apron, and returned to clean off the counter with a wet cloth. She put some dirty glasses into the water bath she had under the counter, and Richard could tell she was avoiding looking him in the face. Though he knew he had said something that she did not like, he asked again if she would go out on a date with him. She replied very fast, "No, I don't think so. I don't date people I don't know. Please don't ask me again." So, said good-bye and left.

Grace felt tears run down her face again, as they had many times before. She thought her life was worthless, that she had disgraced her family by getting pregnant out of wedlock. And then the bastard whom she loved so much left her and the baby and headed for America. She was still living in hopes he would send for her and the child. She gave up watching for the mailman in hopes he might have a letter from America addressed to her. She distanced herself from her child and lived as if the child were her sister. That's what her mother wanted. Her mother was protecting Grace in hopes she would meet a nice man and get married. But with her baggage, he would more than lightly take off.

A-few Days later, Richard returned to the pub where Liam and Peter greeted him at the door. Liam, "Hello, Richard, I see you must like the Guinness here or is there something else here you like?" Peter, "Liam put your ignorance in your pocket, and leave this man alone. Liam, "Richard, I was just joking. Why don't you sit with us, and we can drink and chat." Richard, "Can't right now; I'm in a hurry. Maybe some other time."

Richard went to the counter and asked Grace if he could talk to her in private for a few minutes. Grace, "I'll be right with you as soon as I draw a

few pints of Guinness for those people over here."
Richard stood back a little and waited until she
asked him to come inside the counter and to follow
her to the kitchen at the back. Once in the kitchen,
Richard said, "Grace, I am so sorry for what
happened last time we talked. I know this is a small
community, and people do gossip a lot. I just heard
from someone who came to my butcher shop about
you. They said you had a baby born out of wedlock,
and that put me thinking as to what I might have
said the last time we talked. I could not sleep too
well thinking about what I might have said to upset
you. I pulled every word apart piece by piece, and
finally came up with what I think might have upset
you. I said, 'I had no kids.' If it was that, I'm sorry.
I had no idea at the time you had a child. Please
forgive me, and please reconsider having that date
with me. I would love to date you. I think you are
special, and I have a feeling that you and I were
meant to date. So please reconsider. I have to run
now. I left a friend minding the butcher shop for

me." As Richard was leaving, Liam stood up and whined, "Richard, what's the matter, we are not good enough to have a drink with?" Shamus scolded, "For Christ's sake, Liam, shut up and sit down; you are half drunk." Richard smiled, "Thanks, Shamus. We will have a drink next time. Take care and make sure Liam gets home OK."

Sunday morning Richard decided to go to Mass at the same church that Grace attended. So, he arrived on his bicycle a little early and stood across the road from the school house where the Mass was being said. He was all dressed up in suit and tie. After he put his bike up against the wall, he was approached by a tall man who greeted him, "Hello, perhaps you're a stranger here since I've never seen you before. My name is Gerald. I just moved to this area a few years ago when I married a girl from nearby." "Nice to meet you, Gerald, my name is Richard. I moved to the area a month ago. Tell me, how do you like this place?" "It's really nice,

Richard. The people are very friendly, and they could not do enough for you, if you are ever in need. They are more than happy to help, not like where I came from in the city. There people walk over you and never say 'Hello'. By the way, Richard, where do you come from?" "I come from the east of the city, a country area where my dad has a small farm." "I had to leave the city, Richard, since my wife would not or could not put up with the hustle and bustle. She is such a nice quiet girl. We have one daughter, two years old and the light of our life. The doctor said something's wrong with my wife's insides, and we can't have any more. How about you, are you married?" "No, Gerald, I'm having a hard time finding a nice girl." Gerald chortled, "Richard, maybe we could have a Guinness after Mass in the pub across the street, but for now we had better go in and find a seat. I see the priest coming in his pony and trap, and he likes to see all the people sitting down when he arrives. He is a good man, though a little rough when it comes to giving you penance after confessions. Richard, I usually sit in the second to the last row. It gets a little warm-up front, and sometimes the priest might point his finger at you during the sermon if he is trying to make a point.

They sat next to each other in the second to the last row, and as they were waiting for the priest, Richard shuffled a bit when he saw Grace walk up to sit in one of the front seats. Since they were close to the door, when Mass was over they were the first out. They went across the street for their bicycles and then headed for the bar. Outside the bar there were a few tables where Richard and Gerald sat down at a table and waited for the pub to open in a half-hour or so. As they watched the people leave the church, Gerald repeated, "Now, Richard, I think you are going to like this area. The people are very nice. Look at them chatting over by the wall. I never saw that in the city. It's like they have not seen each other for years. Richard, look at that girl coming towards us. Her name is Grace, a delightful barmaid in the pub here. People like her make you feel welcome." Richard said that he had introduced himself to her, and found her very nice. When the door to the pub opened, Gerald ordered two pints and greeted Grace. He encouraged Grace, "You should come over to my table and meet my friend Richard. Like myself, he is a blow-in to this area." Grace nodded, "Thanks, I already met him." Gerald carried the two pints of Guinness over to the table and sat down. He said to Richard, "She's very nice, but a little tough and a little shy. It would be grand if you two could get together. However, for some reason, it seems she is not interested in dating, from what I hear. I wonder why? She is a very good-looking girl, and she should be married." Richard shrugged that marriage is not for everyone. "But, Richard, she is so pretty."I know, Gerald. That was a tasty pint; let me get the next two."

Richard went over to the counter, smiled at Grace, and asked, "Could I please have two pints and a date?" She answered, "Sure," took the money, and turned around to put it in the till. He thought she did not hear the last part about the date, so he tried again, "Excuse me, Grace, did you hear what I said?" Without turning around she said, "How about tonight after we close the pub?" He radiated, "Sure, I will be outside waiting for you." He took the two pints of Guinness over to the table, and Gerald inquired, "Richard, are you ok? You look like you've seen a ghost." "I'm fine, Gerald, and thanks for inviting me in for the drink. I must be leaving now. I need to open my butcher shop for a few hours. Customers will be waiting for the door to open. Oh, by the way, Gerald, Grace is a really fine girl, and I do have a date with her." "God bless you both. I look forward to us meeting again. You might you come over to my house for dinner sometime and bring Grace with you. This way you can meet my wife. She is a great cook."

Chapter 11

The Barmaid Dates Richard

Later that night Richard rode his bicycle to the pub and waited outside until closing time. Sure enough, Grace showed up nicely dressed in a black skirt and white top. She had on a little lipstick and some rouge upon her cheeks. Richard and Grace chatted for some time as they walked up the main drag from the pub. Instead of discussing the fact that Grace had a child, they chatted about family and their siblings. Grace said her dad was in America for some time and worked as a miner. He contracted black lung and returned home. He had saved up some money and bought the pub where I work. She also said she had two brothers and three sisters. Richard, on the other hand, told her he had a few brothers and two sisters and her that one sister had died at a young age. Grace said one of her sisters also died young. Remarkably, they both died from tuberculosis about the same age.

They turned on to the Boreen that leads to the water where they exchanged more information about themselves. Grace told him she had two sisters, but they were working in the city, one in the hospital and the other in a doctor's office. She broke the ice a little by telling him that sometimes love is a curse. "I fell in love with the father of my child, and look what happened. I disgraced my family, and I know people talk about me behind my back. I could have a job in the hospital or as a secretary for some firm in the city. But I ended up becoming a barmaid. I wanted to help my dad out, and stay home so I could see my baby more often. It's so hard to look at my child and not be able to hug her and tell her who she is. She is a happy child.

"There is no future being a barmaid. You hear all kinds of stories from the patrons as they talk about their neighbors behind their backs. I know they talk about me but not to my face. They pretend to be my friends, but I just listen. I wish I could get to hell away from here. I need someone to tell me what to do. I am so pissed at Shannon's father the bastard. Why did he do this to me and take off? And he called himself a Catholic. We used to sometimes sit in the same seat in church." Richard empathized, "Don't worry. You are a very pretty girl, and you will find someone one day. Then you will have a better life." She sighed, "I hope so. You know you are the first man I went out with since the bastard left. But I can tell you I feel a lot better for having met you. You are so understanding, and I like that. It's very hard to find someone to talk to and share your life's stories. I find it so easy with you. How about your family? Do they have skeletons in closets? I hope not."

Richard told Grace that he had a few brothers in America, and one owned a dance band. The others were somewhere in America as well, but they never write home, and he had no idea where they are. He said his mother worries about them just like your mother worries about you. So many sons and daughters leave home, and for some reason they never look back. It might be that they had to work so hard here for very little money. Richard said his father works very hard, but being married and having a family he could not leave home. "I heard him say to a neighbor one time that he wished he had traveled before he got married and settled down. Some of our neighbors go to England for a few months out of the year. They work in factories and send the money home to feed the family and pay whatever few bills they might have. That's why I left home. I was looking forward to making a better life for myself and hopefully, find a nice girl to marry and raise a family." Richard could see that sharing some family history was raising Grace's spirits. He could tell she had been in a rut but was now starting to smile a little more. Finally, Grace asked Richard to come to dinner the following Saturday at her house. Richard said he would love

to because he knew he would get a home-cooked
meal which he had not had in a long time.

When Grace told her mother about Richard, her
mother was excited to see that after so many years
Grace was starting to smile. She looked happier
than she had seen her in a long time. Grace swept
the flagstone floor, and washed the dishes to be
used that night. She turned the table cloth over,
putting the good side up on the table. Grace's
mother greeted Richard with open arms when he
arrived. Grace's two brothers, Frank and Griffin,
soon arrived in from the field. When Frank asked
Richard if he would like a drink, Richard said,
"Sure, as long as it's not buttermilk." In the
meantime, Grace went over to the two pots hanging
by hooks over the open fire and removed the covers
from both. They were filled with potatoes. The
small pot held large potatoes for the dinner, and the
other pot the little ones for the fowl and pigs. Frank
left the house for a short time, and returned carrying

a bottle of clear liquid. Richard smiled since he knew it was poteen in the bottle.

Griffin went to the dresser and took down three egg stands for use as shot glasses while Frank poured the poteen with a steady hand lest he spill a drop. They tipped the egg stands, and Frank said, "Slainte," meaning good health. Richard downed the drink and smacked his lips. He had never tasted poteen so good, and to think that Grace had told him there was none to be had. When they sat down to dinner, Grace put on the table a small basket filled with potatoes, a large platter with a hunk of bacon, another plate with country butter, and another with onions, boiled carrots, and parsnips-a meal fit for a king. Frank told Richard to sit at the end of the table. Grace filled a plate for her mother who wanted to sit by the open fire. Frank was telling Richard about his day in the field, and before they were finished, Callahan and his brother Brady arrived. They had been working all day in the bog cutting turf. Grace introduced everyone, and her father seemed very comfortable with Richard, welcoming him as if he were his own son. Grace set a place for them at the table, and they sat down to eat. Frank, as the oldest of the children, got up and went to the churn where he filled two big mugs of buttermilk and set them down in from of him and Griffin, and two more for Callahan and Brady. Callahan asked Richard what he did for a living. Richard told him that he had rented a shop and was doing some butchering.

Callahan informed Richard that if he ever want to buy sheep or lambs for the slaughter, he would be glad to sell him some. When dinner was over, they all sat on chairs before the fire. Richard started getting nervous, wondering if they were going to grill him about his life. Callahan asked Richard what brought him to the area, and he replied that when he had served in the Irish army, he had spent some time traveling through the area,

and he fell in love with the next town. "I'm sure
you met Grace here in the pub. She is my right-hand
person: not only is she my daughter, but also my
secretary and, of course, the best barmaid in the
county." (Oh boy, this is not going too well!) "Yes,
I met her in your pub where she drew me one of the
finest pints of Guinness I ever had, and I have had
many." Callahan continued, "Grace is the best
barmaid and the most caring daughter a father could
ask for. Frank, why don't you get a drop of the
creature, and we will click our egg stands and toast
our new friend Richard." "Now that's better,"
Richard thought. Frank poured a few eggs stands
full and passed them around, and Callahan toasted
their new friend Richard. "This was just the start of
the interrogation," Richard imagined.

Callahan, "So you fancy Grace. I'm sure otherwise
you would not be here. He could tell the family was
in a protective mode. And he could see why. A
short time later, a young girl entered the house. She

had been visiting her cousins next door. She went over and sat on the arm of Alanna's chair.

Alanna said, "Shannon, I want you to meet Richard. He is a friend of Grace. "Oh, is he going to marry her?" "This is not going well at all," Richard privately concluded. He stood up and excusing himself said thanks for dinner, and that he hoped to visit again sometime, please God. "I must go now it's quite a way to my shop. Tomorrow morning, I have to slaughter a few lambs and set up shop for the day."

Grace spoke up, "Richard, I will walk with you to the gate. They held hands as they chatted and Grace told him about Shannon and who she was. "Shannon thinks I am her sister; that's how my mother and father wanted it." When Richard asked why Shannon's father left, she explained that he claimed in America he could make a better life for her and Shannon. You are the first person I have dated since he left. "I was so much in love with the guy," but she never mentioned his name. "I don't think he loved me at all. I think he was a con artist, and I was gullible. He got what he wanted and left. I was so stupid and caused so many problems for everyone. I should have listened to my mother, who always said only to spread your legs to pee. I have never heard from him, and I have no idea where he is in America. I know he went to some relatives there. Sometimes I wish he would rot in hell. Although I can't really blame him for destroying my life, I did that myself."

Richard held Grace's hand as they walked to the gate, and he could feel the hurt she was going through. He was falling in love with her, but this was not the time or place to tell her that. They did not kiss. He set off on his bicycle. They set a time for their next date later in the week. Richard went to his shop and did some thinking. He started wondering if he should run away now before he got too deep into the relationship. He needed to talk to someone and share his story about Grace with them, but it had to be the right person. Next morning was Monday. He got up early and slathered a few sheep, hung them up on hooks to the overhead bar in the shop, and wrapped them in muslin to keep the flies off the meat. He opened up his shop and had a very busy day. He decided to take the next day off and go visit his mother and brother. He posted a sign in the window that read "Closed Today".

Chapter 12

Advice from a Mother

Early next morning Richard rode his bicycle to the train. He was allowed to carry his bicycle into the last car. After the short train ride, he rode his bicycle three miles to his mother's house. He walked into his mother's kitchen shouting, "Anyone home?" When he found his mother was out back getting some turf for the fire, she greeted him, "My God, Richard, your home, give me a hand to bring in some turf. I have no idea where your brother Noel has gone. He was there a minute ago. He can disappear like a ghost in the night. Richard, how are you doing? How is the butcher shop working out? Are you selling much meat? Do you need some money? My God, take off that shirt, and I will wash it for you. When did you change it last? Richard, you must be hungry. Sit, and I will get you something to eat. I think it's time you settled down. Why don't you find a nice girl who will put the skids under you, and you will be much happier?"

Now this one-sided conversation was going very well. He was getting advice and answers without asking any questions.   "Richard! Have you heard anything I said? Where the hell is that other son of mine gone? He is as lazy as sin. All he wants to do all day is play with his accordion, and then he's out all night. He says he plays in a band somewhere. I will say one thing; he never asks for money. By the way, Richard, how are you for money? Are you eating all right, you look like you lost a few pounds? I hope you are not getting sick.   Your sister started to lose weight before she died, may God rest her soul. I miss her so much. She was such a good girl; never gave   your father or me any trouble. Some girls get into a lot of trouble mind you. Ann Coffee over the road, poor thing went missing, and they have not found her. Some man put her in the family way. Sure, she might have gone to England or someplace. They say her father beat her up and kicked her out of the house when he found out. What a shame. Richard! Tell me, have you met any nice girl in that town you moved to? Sure, there must be plenty of good girls around. Not all girls are bad, but then you might be hard to please.

"Where in the hell is that son of mine? Richard, look out by the haggard, and see if he is out there. Look at the back of the house, and see if his bicycle is gone. If it's gone, he must be over to Hardy's house. Sometimes Hardy plays with him in a band. Sit, and I will fry you some bacon and eggs. Your father went to the Bog today to bring home a cartload of turf.   Your brother should have gone with him, but he is so lazy. He's not like you. You were always very helpful before you left to join the army. Will you get any kind of a pension from the army?" "No, mom, I won't get any pension. That's for people that make a career out of it like twenty years or so." "I hear your brother coming now whistling as usual." "Noel!" "Well, if it isn't my big brother Richard come home to roost! How are you, Richard? You the very person I need to talk to. I just came from having a chat with Harvey over the road, and he wants us to start up our own band. What do you think?" "Well, Noel, I'm not the best one to give advice right now. I myself am looking for advice." "And you came to me?" "No, I came to talk to our mother. I think I got the answers to all my questions without asking one." "And what might that be, Richard?" "Let us go out to the haggard and chat." "Richard, this is not like you. You were always one to chat in front of everyone, so this must be serious?" "Noel, I met this girl, and I think I am falling for her." "Come on, Richard; this is getting juicier by the minute. There's got to be more. You did not come all the way to tell us you might be falling for a girl. Come on, tell me the rest.

"Did you get her in trouble, you dirty old man?"
"No, I did not. Let's be serious for now. Someone
else got her in trouble five or six years ago, and she
has a daughter." "Oh, my God, did you tell mother
this?" "No, I did not tell mother this. She was just
telling me about Ann Coffee over the road. Do you
have any idea where she went to?" "Well, rumor
has it she is pregnant, and her father beat the crap
out of her and ordered her to leave the house. The
priest sent her to a home run by the nuns.   I'm
sure she will be OK. Why do you ask?" "Well, the
girl I met was not put into a home, she was not
beaten by her father, and the father and mother are
raising the child as if she were their own daughter."
"Richard, I think that is great, and I wish others
would do the same. I hear those poor girls are
treated very badly in those homes." "Noel, I think I
have my answer. Oh, by the way that's a good idea
about getting a band going. This way you can sleep
all day." "Mother, I will have some of that dinner
you promised me, and then I will be off. I do have a

business to run. And I don't want to miss the last
train."

Chapter 13

Richard Passes a Note to Grace

The next day Richard was very busy in the shop. He had to slaughter and fleece two more sheep and one lamb since there were so many guests in the town that day to attend the receptions for two weddings. Richard waited until Friday night to go visit the pub and see Grace. As usual Liam and his friends were there. This time he did not buy them a drink, but went up to the counter, passed a note to Grace, and left. Grace went into the back room before reading the note.

"Dear Grace, I have been very busy these past few days, but I have some time tomorrow evening. Can you meet me down by the waterfall, and we can chat. I'll be there around 7:00 P.M. If you don't show up, I will understand."

Richard arrived at 6:30 P.M. he was puffing on a cigarette as if it were his last. Sure enough, he spotted Grace in the distance walking towards him. His heart skipped a beat. He somehow knew his life was going to take a turn for the better. Grace and Richard sat down on a rock next to the waterfall and held hands. They did not talk much at the beginning. It seemed by holding hands they could feel their minds were talking to each other, and for some reason, when Richard did start to say something, Grace also started by saying the very same word. They stood up and kissed, and then walked towards the waterfall where they removed their shoes and sat on a rock with their feet under the running water. "Richard, you are the first person I went out with since the father to my child abandoned her and me. Sometimes I get really pissed at him, but then again, it takes two the tango. However, I think I was the winner. Her father lost out because I love looking at my daughter, even though I cannot give her a hug other than a sisterly hug, and sure, there is a difference. At times I just wanted to tell her I was her mother, but my mother would say, 'Now, child, will you leave things the way they are. Its best for all concerned.' There must be a reason my mother did not want me to tell her. Maybe one day she will tell me. Shannon's father had a nice smile, and I thought we were so much in love. He must have been a con artist; he did not care anything for me. He got what he wanted and left. I was stupid. I have not really lived these past few years. I am even a bit hesitant about striking up any kind of a relationship. You are the first man I have dated since he took off."

"Grace, it's getting late. Let me walk you home, and we'll have another date in a few days." She answered she would like that.

Richard went home and could not get Grace out of his mind. He tossed in the bed which was not too comfortable to begin with. He had bought it from a hawker Fair Day in the town. The next day he went to another pub in town for a few drinks, and that's when he made up his mind, He said to himself, "My mother is right. I need to settle down, but not just to have someone to do my laundry and cook for me; I can do that for myself. I think Grace is the person I want to be with for the rest of my life."

Next day, Friday, he got up early and set up all the meat needed for his customers for the weekend. It was a long day since he was looking forward to seeing Grace at the pub that evening. He always kept his bicycle outside the back door against the wall, but when he went out, it was not there. He thought to himself that some bastard must have stolen it. Then he remembered that he had taken it into the shop the night before due to the thunder and lighting. When he pushed it outside, however, he discovered there was a flat tire on the front wheel. He started wondering if God was sending him a message. He turned the bicycle upside down on the floor, took two spoons from the table, and opened the side of the tire from the rim. Then he pulled out the tube, pumped in some air to locate the leak, cleaned the spot, and put a repair patch over the hole. He put it all back together and headed off to the pub.

On his way he saw ahead of him a pony and trap stopped crossways on the road, with the pony eating grass along the side the road. Since there was a person sitting sideways in the trap, Richard got off his bicycle and walked over to the trap to check it out. There was Liam fast asleep in the trap still holding the reins in one hand, a bottle of Guinness in the other, and his head resting on the top rim of the trap. Richard shook Liam a few times and said, "Come on, Liam, wake up. It's time to go to the pub." Liam said, "I'll be right with you; wait for me," and went back to sleep. Richard walked alongside the pony, pushing his bicycle with one hand and holding on to the bridle by the other. They stopped outside the pub where Richard tied the rains

to the gate. Inside the pub, Richard met Peter and
Shamus and told them that Liam was outside
waiting to take them home.

Richard smiled at Grace. She was behind the
counter. She smiled back at him. He then looked
over towards the table in the corner and noticed
George sitting by himself with a full pint, and a shot
glass filled with whiskey sitting on the table.
Richard went over and said to George, "Do you
mind if I sit down?" George replied, "Go right
ahead. My name is George. What's yours?" "They
call me Richard. I have seen you a few times over
there with Liam and his friends. They drink too
much; don't you think?" "Richard, thanks for sitting
with me. I would like to ask you a question. Where
are you from originally? I know you're not our type
of people because you don't look like a drinker."
"Well, George, I guess we all have our drinking
times depending on what's going on in our lives."
"Richard, let me tell you this. I am having some

problems at home with my wife. I thought we were happy until a few weeks ago when she started to pick on little things I was doing. She became very silent and will not discuss anything with me. She spends hours talking to my son and two daughters. One of my daughters was going out with a blow in, and he seemed like a very nice lad, but then you can't judge the book by the cover. All of a sudden, he vanished. When I asked my daughter where he went and what happened, she did not answer me; she just started to cry. I asked my wife Peg where he went, and it seems she knows something and will not talk about it.

Richard commented, "You mentioned that her boyfriend vanished. George, if you don't mind me saying this, I think you should sit down with your daughter and in a nice way tell her you are worried about her. Tell her not to be afraid to talk because, after all, you are her father. Ask her if there something wrong, and would she like to talk to you about it. You can also tell her that there is no problem that can't be fixed. Be a good listener. She might open up and tell you what is going on in her life." Richard wondered if the girl might be pregnant.

 "George, you should also ask your wife to sit down and tell you what is going on. Tell her you care a lot for her. She might be worried about you and your drinking." "Sure, Richard, I would not be drinking if they would only talk to me." George downed the shot of whiskey followed by a slug from the pint, and said, "Richard, many thanks for listening to me. I'm going home now to tell my wife we have to talk".

Chapter 14

Richard Asks Grace to Marry Him

Richard went to the counter and smiled at Grace. She could tell that Richard was different from others, more understanding and the type of man she would like to marry. She thought she could be very happy with him. She drew a pint for Richard and said, "I'll see you in a few hours down by the waterfall." She had a tickling, exciting feeling in her stomach every time she looked at Richard.

Richard took his pint and sat down next to Shamus at the table. Shamus inquired, "Where in the hell did you find Liam and the pony?" Richard replied, "Back the road a bit. Sure he must be coming from the Widow Mitchell's house. I think they have a thing going.

She likes her hot Toddies." Shamus said, "She must like more than that. Richard, how is the business doing? I have a few lambs for sale. Would you be interested in taking them off my hands?" "Sure, Shamus, next time you are up my way drop them off. If I'm not there, leave them in the outside pin in the rear of the shop."

The door opened, and this tall well-built man walked in. It was Grace's dad. Everyone's head turned towards him, and the customers agreed, "Sure, the next round of drinks will be on the house." The man was Callahan, a very likable easy going man. He came over to Richard's and Shamus's table and sat down next to Richard. "Well, how are you boys doing tonight? Be careful; don't drink too much. Sometimes it can mean the end of a marriage."

Sure, Callahan saw lots in his life. When he started telling stories about his time in America, he chose his topic very carefully about when he worked in the mines. He would have Liam and his friends from the bar around him, and would cough a little as if to tell you why he came home. He never mentioned black lung. I guess he thought that was a deadly disease, and if he did not mention it, it would go away. He walked up to the counter and whispered something to Grace. Then he came back and sat down, this time next to Shamus. We heard Grace shout this round of drinks is on the house. Everyone in unison shouted, "Thanks, Callahan." Grace came to the table with drinks, a medium for her father and a pint each for Shamus and Richard. Callahan remarked, "I don't come here too often, Grace takes care of the bar. I like to walk across the few fields I own, and look over the few live stock. Sometimes Grace needs a break, so I stop in, and she can take some time off. Richard was happy to see Callahan go inside the counter, and see Grace take off her apron."

Richard left through the front door, and Grace through the back door from the kitchen. They met at the gable end of the pub, and headed towards the waterfall where they held hands, kissed, and talked. Grace was nervous, but not as much as Richard. Their hands were sweaty when Grace asked, "Richard, are you OK? You seemed nervous." "Yes, I am. Would you get nervous if I asked you to marry me?" She gasped, "Oh my God, yes! Did you just ask me to marry you?" Richard nodded, "I did." "Oh my God, yes; I will marry you! I was hoping you would ask me. I used to dream of marrying a man like you, so good and understanding. Yes, oh yes, I will marry you!"

She stood up took a few steps towards the waterfall. She listened to the sound of the water as it rushed over the rocks, and it was as if the sound was saying, "Yes, I will. Yes, I will." She turned around, and there was Richard facing her. He had sneaked up on her. Again, He heard yes I will yes I will. They kissed and kissed some more. Then they took off their shoes, sat on a rock, and put their feet into the running water. They held hands and were silent.

Then Richard spoke up as though in command. "Grace, I have given this a lot of thought over the past few weeks, and I think we should talk about your daughter. What is going to happen to her? I think we should talk with her and tell her the truth, rather than have her believe she is your sister. Grace answered, "I have spoken to the priest many times in hopes he could help me make a decision as to what to do. I thought it would help me to feel less guilty about what I did wrong. It was his opinion that because I was an innocent at the time, I did nothing wrong and my mother and father did the right thing by raising the child as their own. In years to come when she finds out the truth, hopefully she will be able to forgive me. Richard, thanks for thinking of her. I only wish I could be closer to her and tell her the truth, but everyone seems to know better than me. Now are you sure you want to marry me? And that it's not because you are feeling sorry for me?" "Grace, I somehow knew

I wanted to marry you from that first day you filled that first pint of Guinness for me. Now when do we tell your parents?" "Why don't you come to dinner at my house tomorrow, and we can tell them? My mother is always home and I will make sure my dad is home as well."

Richard did not sleep to well that night thinking about getting married, where to live, Grace's daughter, money which he did not have, and many other things kept his head spinning. "Am I crazy? Why did my mother plant the seed in my mind, is God telling me something, will I be a good spouse?" Richard woke up early next morning, and made himself a cup of tea into which he poured a shot of whiskey. He rearranged some meats he had in his butcher shop, and reduced the prices on some. He counted whatever money he had both in his pockets and in the till. Not too much, but he was debt free. He went into the bedroom, knelt down next to his bed, and prayed for guidance. He was raised Catholic, and his mother had emphasized that if you're ever in trouble, talk to God. Well, he was not in trouble this time, but he is sure as hell needed a friend to tell him he was doing the right thing. He wanted to be assured that all would be OK.

Next day Richard set off on his bicycle and arrived at Grace's house where he was met by Grace at the gate. They kissed, and Grace said, "My dad will be here shortly. He left a half-hour ago to drive the two cows back to the field after their morning milking. Come in and say hello to my mother." Richard entered the kitchen, and Grace's mother greeted him, "Nice to see you again Richard. Pull up a chair sit and rest your bones." Richard sat on a chair next to Grace's mom, and she held out her hand to welcome him. She continued, "Grace will have dinner ready soon; you must be hungry. Grace, why don't you pour Richard a drink?" Then Callahan entered and came over to Richard to shake his hand. "I saw your bicycle by the gate. It looks new. How are you doing, and the butcher shop? I spoke with Shamus a short time ago. He was saying that he dropped off a few lambs at your place this morning, but you were not home. Shamus is a very good man and very honest. Callahan invited Richard to sit at the table, and tell him a little about himself.

Grace had the table set for four. She placed two jugs filled with buttermilk one on each end of the table and two more filled with Guinness which she placed in the center of the table. She also put out two platters, one filled with potatoes and the other with bacon and cabbage. Callahan invited everyone to sit-down and eat. He poured buttermilk into his glass and offered some to Richard. "No thanks, I'll have a Guinness, if you please. It goes better with bacon and cabbage." Alannah was not saying much, but you could tell she had her ear cocked and was doing her fair share of listing. She spoke up, "Grace, sit down at the table and eat. Sure, you are killed working. I wonder where Shannon is?" "Mom, she went next door to visit Julie and is having dinner with her. You know that child never stays home; she is away visiting the neighbors." Callahan inquired, "Richard, have you met my youngest daughter Shannon yet? She is such a sweet girl she's going to be seven years old in a few weeks." " No Sir, I have not met her yet, but I am looking forward to meeting her." Grace put some dinner on a plate and took it over to Alannah who liked to eat by the fire.

When dinner was over, they pulled their chairs down around the fire while Grace cleared the table. The kettle was boiling over the fire, and Grace put some loose tea into the teapot and filled it with water just off the boil. She placed in on a few hot coals by the fire. A short time later, she filled the cups and handed a cup to her mom, dad, and Richard. Grace sat down next to Richard. She was very nervous and wondered how her family would react when they were told the news about her and Richard getting married. Richard got up and placed his cup on the table and then stood between Callahan and the fire. He cleared his throat and asked Grace to stand next to him. As she reached out her hand to hold his, Grace glowed, "Richard and I would like your blessing. Richard has asked me to marry him, and I said, 'Yes'." Callahan jumped up, pushed his chair way back to the table, and going over to Alannah, held her hands lifting her from the chair. "Alannah, did you hear that? Grace is getting married." Callahan, "Why are we drinking Tea? This calls for a fresh bottle of poteen." As he filled one egg-stand after another and passed them around, he said, "Richard, you make me the happiest man in the world today. Alannah, you have always made me happy. Let us drink a toast to Richard and Grace. Wait until the rest of her siblings hear the good news. There will be dancing in this house tonight to celebrate." Callahan was so excited because he knew what others did not know. He felt he had only a few years to live because of the black lung decease. He was not one to complain.

Richard and Grace walked towards the gate where they kissed and hugged. "Richard, you go home, rest up, and be back here again later this evening. If I know my dad, this house will be filled with all the neighbors and gallons of poteen and Guinness. Richard we are going to have a great life together, and I will be a good spouse and care for you." As Richard rode his bicycle up the narrow road, he was blocked by some cattle two men were driving his way. He got off the bicycle, carried it to the wall, and waited until the cattle went by. The two men and Richard greeted each other. He could tell they were in a hurry, and found out later they were Grace's brothers.

Chapter 15

Grace Is Seldom Wrong.

Richard decided to wash, shave, and dress properly in hopes that Grace might be right. He arrived on his bicycle, and could hear the music a half-mile away. He didn't know how Callahan managed to get all those people in such a short space of time. People young and old packed the house and yard. Two violins, two accordions, two tin whistles, and, of course, a mouth organ provided the music.

Richard was stopped by two lads at the gate. One took his bicycle and the other asked him to follow him around to the shed through a small field and then to the cow shed. He asked Richard to wait in the cowshed until Callahan came to fetch him. Richard was nervous and felt like running away. He could not believe the racket that was going on in the house. Callahan arrived at the cow-house all done up in his Sunday best. It was a suit that somehow survived in the pillow case he took home from America.

He shook Richard's hand and said, "Come on future son-in-law, follow me." Callahan entered the kitchen grinning from ear to ear; you could tell he was a happy man. There was silence. Then someone shouted, "What the hell is going on here; did someone die?" Everyone took a good look at Callahan all dressed up in his Sunday best. Callahan announced, "You arrived here this evening thinking we were just having a shindig and a few drinks, but take a good look at me. Do I get dressed up like this for a shindig? I put on my best suit, the only suit I have, so I could introduce you all to my future son-in-law." He then asked Richard to come in and stand next to him. "I want you to meet Richard, the best butcher in the area, who is going to marry my daughter Grace. I want silence now so you can all hear me. Alannah and I are the happiest parents today as we give our first-born child, also known as "The Irish Barmaid," to Richard here. Now Richard, let me introduce my friends, some of whom you know from the pub. Tonight the pub is closed. You are all here for free Guinness and whiskey."

Everyone stood up and started clapping. They asked Richard and Grace to take the center floor. The music started and someone shouted, "We know Grace can dance; let's see if

Richard can dance!" The music was a waltz to which Richard and Grace spun across the flagstone floor as if they were spinning tops. Grace was ecstatic, "You never told me you could dance." "Sure," he said, "I love to dance, and I love music."

When the music stopped, Shamus sitting on the hob by the fire, shouted, "How about a song from Liam over there?" Liam protested, "I'm not a good singer; ask Peter." Peter held off, "I'm not drunk enough yet; maybe later. Why not get Grace's talented brothers to sing." Francis sang followed by his brother Griffin. They got loud applause and cries of "That a boy; what a pair of lungs."

There were so many people outside hoping to get in that the house could not accommodate. Someone yelled from the back, "Let's all be quiet now. Shamus here heard some gossip about Richard." Oh boy, was there silence! Then, "Gossip! Is it good or bad gossip?" Seamus was invited to the center of the floor where someone handed him a glass of Guinness. He cleared his throat, "I heard that Richard here is a champion step-dancer." "Come on now, who did you hear that from?" "I met a man today in Molloy's pub. He was passing through and came from the east of here and knows Richard's family well. He told me

they were a nice family, and that he had seen Richard's dance
one time at a festival."

Callahan asked Richard to honor them with a dance, and
Tim to play a tune for Richard. Richard asked for a hornpipe.
Shamus told everyone to push back and give Richard the floor.
Tim pulled his chair out so the crowd could see him play, and
Richard danced the hornpipe with taps to the beat of the music
that only a champion could make. Richard had metal tips on the
heels and toes of his shoes which sounded great on the flagstone
floor as the sparks flew in all directions. When Richard finished
the dance, Grace came over and gave him a big hug that got
bigger applause than the dance. Callahan took the center floor
and asked the guests to fill their glasses. "Now let's raise them
high and we will give a toast to the happy couple, and the
second toast will be to me and my darling Alannah here."

Callahan congratulated Richard and Grace and shook their
hands warmly. "I am a happy man tonight. I spoke with Grace
this evening, and she is a changed woman. She said, 'God sent
her an angel when she really needed one.'" The dance lasted
most of the night, and finally Richard said to Grace, "I must go
home now. I have customers I must care for tomorrow with a

line at my shop door looking for bacon, sausages, and eggs.

Grace walked Richard to the gate, and they hugged, kissed, and

Richard headed off on his bicycle.

Chapter 16

Grace and Richard Get Married.

The morning of the wedding everyone was running from one room to the other, filling Callahan's house to an uproar of joy, tears, and laughter. While shoes were getting polished, you could smell the rashers as they sizzled on the pan. Grace was searching for the few items that belonged to her, piling them in the middle of the floor. Callahan came in after milking the two cows, removing his wellingtons which had cow dung on them and placing them next to the fire. In a short time, all were nicely dressed in their Sunday best. Grace gathered up her few items off the floor, put them into a cardboard box, and handed them to Brady. As they were going out the door, Callahan asked if the dog had been fed. When no one answered, Callahan had to go back and feed the "poor dog", as he would say.

Callahan's brother drove them in the same sidecar to the same church to which some years before he had driven his brother Callahan. Brady stopped the horse outside Richard's butcher shop so Grace could drop off her few items of clothing.

The door was unlocked and Grace put the box of items on the floor in the back room which was a mess. Richard must be at the church already. They arrived outside the church and the crowd of people standing around started waving and shouting, "We are so happy for you." Grace was wondering if all those church-going hypocrites knew about her past. Gossip travels fast in a small area, and what they were happy about was that some stupid man would marry her. Callahan and Alannah had face-creasing smiles. As they held hands, Callahan asked, "Remember when you walked up this aisle with your father walking beside you?" She answered, "Yes, and I wonder if he loved me like we love Grace." Callahan, the proud father, asked Grace if she were ready to take the big step. She radiated, "Yes, daddy." He walked up the aisle, back straight and linking his arm with his daughter's. Alannah followed, holding onto Shannon's hand, and then the rest of the family. They all sat in the front rows of seats.

Suddenly, there was the sound of an automobile horn outside the church. A man walked up the aisle past the altar and stood beside Richard who was standing by the sacristy door. It was his brother Bartley whom Richard had asked to be his best man. Seconds later, as a further surprise for all, a beautiful girl walked up the aisle, hugged Grace, and stood next to her. It was her sister Nellie who worked in the hospital, and whom Grace had asked to be her bridesmaid. This was all done in secret as a surprise for Callahan and Alannah. The priest asked those in the church if they would please stand and welcome the rest of Richard's family who had traveled some distance for the wedding. Among them were his mom and dad and, to Richard surprise, one of his brother's home from America. The priest said we are ready to begin the ceremony.

The noise now started as the crowd of people from outside started to rush into the church, all doing their best to sit up front. The music started as their friend Tim started to play soft music on his violin. Callahan handed Grace over to Richard with a handshake, and stepped down from the altar. He sat in the front seat next to Alannah and Shannon. The music from Tim's violin brought tears to the congregants' eyes as he played all the hymns. The priest gave a very fine speech after he pronounced them man and wife. He said, "May God give them good health and bless them with many children." He finished with, "If I know Callahan, there will be clear liquid flowing in his bar this evening." The priest was new to the area and did not know all the gossip that was traveling among people, but he would find out fast. Sure, everyone tells him what's happening in the area when they go to confession. It's a way to talk freely when your face is covered.

Outside the church Richard and Grace were surrounded by their friends telling them how nice they looked on the altar. Brady had a wooden box nicely painted which he placed on the ground as a foot stool so people could step up onto his sidecar. When Brady stopped by Richard's shop on the way so the front door could be locked, Callahan encouraged Richard and Grace to spend some time in the shop until Brady picked them up later. That would give him time to set up for "a very small party we might have at the pub this evening." Grace and Richard went into the shop and Brady drove the rest home.

After entering the shop with the door closed, they really had their first passionate kiss as man and wife. Grace offered to make them a cup of tea, and had Richard sit at the table. She poked the fire a little and added some turf and a few kindling pieces to get it going. Then she started to clean up the room and the little kitchen. She was in her glory married to the man she loved. She could feel the difference between their relationship and what she thought was love in her past but was only sexual attraction. Richard, meanwhile, tuned in on a small battery operated radio, and began to dance to the music. Since the place was very small, they ended up dancing into the shop area and around the meat that was hanging by hooks from the steel bar. They stopped and kissed before long, and ended up in the small bed where they consummated their marriage. After she made a fresh cup of tea, they sat at the small table. Richard sat down on the only chair he had with Grace on his knee.

Next thing they heard Brady pounding on the door to tell them it was time to go see what Callahan had in store for them. As Brady sat in the seat facing the horse's rear, he let the end of the whip run gently on the horses back. He did not have to hit her; she knew when to start moving. Brady started to whistle and Richard and Grace held hands as they both sat on one side of the sidecar. Brady stopped the horse, climbed down from his seat, and sat on the other side of the sidecar opposite Richard and Grace, balancing the weight on the sidecar. When they arrived at the pub, there were pony and traps, bicycles, and even an old car parked alongside the road. My God, people were outside and inside the pub, standing room only. Callahan and Alannah were standing at the door, and Shannon ran out to greet the newlyweds. Shannon was so excited since it was her first time at a wedding. She grabbed Grace and hugged her. To Grace this seemed like a different kind of hug, and she could not control her tears as they ran down her cheeks. Richard handed her a hankie. Shannon held on to Grace's hand as they walked to the door where Callahan and Alannah were waiting.

Callahan announced, "Let's clear the way for the newlyweds." The barmaid this time was Grace's sister and she too could draw good pint of Guinness. The glasses were already filled and lined up on the counter with shot glasses in front waiting to be filled depending on who wanted one. Callahan and Alannah took center floor and welcomed the newlyweds. He could not express himself he was so happy so he asked his oldest son to do the honors. They thought he would never stop welcoming Richard into the family. Shamus, who was the watch dog at the window, warned, "Pass the word to hide the clear stuff." Well, the place was still when this stranger walked in. Callahan thought he was a guard on the raid. The stranger, a short little man well dressed and using a walking stick, stood in

the doorway and said, "Am I invited to this great party or not?"
Shamus told him it was a private party and he would have to
leave. "To hell with you; I want to see Callahan. Where is
he?" Callahan walked toward the door, and dropped his full pint
of Guinness glass on the floor. He opened his hands wide and
shouted as he gave one big hug to him. "Porter, my friend,
where in Jesus did you come from? Come in and meet my wife
Alannah and the newlyweds Grace and Richard." Callahan got
his voice back quickly as he introduced Porter to the crowd,
"This is my best friend Porter whom I met on the ship when I
headed for America. He comes from the next village over."
Porter said, "Everyone, carry on with your celebration. I am
going to find a corner, have a pint, and watch the carrying on.

Tim the musician started of the music on his violin
followed by non-other than Shamus who had a comb and a piece
of paper that he somehow blew through and created music. Just
then Richard's brother Bartley appeared in the doorway
followed by four strangers carrying cases in which they had
musical instruments. It was a five-piece band known as
"Harvey's Dance Band". They set up the instruments alongside
Tim and Shamus, and Callahan clapped, "Let the dancing

begin!" Richard and Grace danced gloriously in the center of the floor. Callahan and Porter chatted about what had happened over the past twenty years or so. The party lasted into the small hours of the morning.

Alannah woke up early, poked the fire, and put the kettle on. She looked around for Callahan who was nowhere to be found. She went into a bedroom and found Richard and Grace fast asleep still in their good clothing. She went outside and there were Callahan and Porter sitting at a table chatting away and having a pint in front of them. She told them she would have breakfast in a short time. Porter was filling Callahan in about his time in the mines after he left. "I was now going in what seemed like a few miles underground in a carriage, and some days were better than others. I started to get headaches, and then one day there was an explosion in the mine. All hell broke loose. Men were trapped. A new crew was sent in to do some digging and when they got through seven of the ten crew members were rescued, and walked out to the carriage. The other three were taken out on stretchers. Later that day I was told that they died. After I had cleaned up and went in to have a bite to eat, Redmond Murphy the timekeeper came over to see how I was doing. He had tears in his eyes as he told us that his brother Duff was one of the three that died. In the days that followed with the burial and all, I made up my mind to return to Ireland. So here I am, and you are the first one I looked up after coming home. Callahan, I am staying with a cousin of mine in County Mayo, a long drive from here. Most of my family has died off. My mom and dad died a few years ago, and I will visit their grave before I leave. The brother I gave the boat to when I left for America drowned a few years later. But, my friend, we will keep in touch. No good giving you my address unless you went back to school to learn how to read and write." "Listen, Porter, I have a secretary now who can read and write. She's my lovely wife Alannah; so you can give me your address. Porter had Brady drive him later that day to the train station.

Richard and Grace set up their temporary living quarters at the rear of the butcher shop, and were ever so happy.

Chapter 17

The First Born Grandson

As the months went on, Richard and Grace built up a profitable butcher business. Shamus too did well by selling his lambs and sheep to Richard. Brady would sometimes drive Callahan and Alannah to visit Richard and Grace, and on the way home Callahan would mentioned to Alannah that it would be grand if God blessed them with a child or two.

One year later, they had a baby boy which gave Callahan a reason to have another big party in his pub. For this first grandson Callahan was more excited than the parents, especially since he had thought he might not live to see this day. The party lasted two days, and the barmaid this time was Bridget's sister Olive. She took a few years off from her job at the city, since she was burned out from the hustle and bustle and people's demanding ways. She felt as though she was having a nervous breakdown. She had never dated perhaps from seeing what happened to Bridget and her man taking off to America. That took its toll on everyone at the time.

Callahan would visit Grace and Richard just to play with the baby. He was so delighted. Grace said to Richard, "See how happy my dad is playing with the baby. It's as if he got a new toy for Christmas." A few weeks later, however, while Grace was feeding the baby, there was a knock at the door. Grace's brother Frank walked in sobbing. Grace asked, "What's wrong? Has someone died?" Frank replied, "Daddy died a few hours ago, and I'm on my way to get the priest." Grace said, "I knew he was holding something back the last time he was here playing with the baby. When he left, he was different as if he knew this would be the last time he would see his grandson. He never talked about his black lung disease, but he knew his life would be short. He was so happy to have lived to see his first grandson."

Grace took over as the barmaid for the next two days as Callahan was waked. Mourners came from all over to say goodbye to a great man. Some had stories they had heard from other people about Callahan's past. Several stories were made up, of course. The pub had standing room only until Liam,

Shamus, and Peter came in. Liam pulled out the round table from the corner and set it up, pushing some people out of the way. Grace looked over and asked them if they wanted the usual and then she started to laugh. Her mind drifted back to the times she would ask them if they wanted the usual. They would sit at the same table in the same corner, busting chops with the poor stranger who entered and whom she later married. For a few minutes it eased the pain from losing her dad. A short time later Tom the matchmaker came in followed by Gerald and Brady. Shamus asked for quiet, and said he would like all to raise their glasses in a toast for Callahan who was a friend to everyone. Just as he was about to say something there was a commotion at the door and you could hear a pin drop. Someone asked, "Is it a raid? "

Grace came from behind the counter, and went to the door. Although it was dark by the door, she could see something shining as she looked down. It was a walking stick with a silver ring on the handle, held by none other than Callahan's friend Porter. The crowd cleared a passage from the door to the table where Peter was so Porter could take a seat. Grace pulled a pint for Porter and took it over to him. He was crying as he shook hands with her, and said, "Grace, Callahan was so proud of you. Ever since I went to live in county Mayo, every letter he sent me, written, of course, by your mother, he never forgot to mention your name. He was my friend, and I will miss him. The last time I sat with him here in this pub, his dream in life, he gave me his walking stick with the silver ring on the handle, and now that he is gone I want you to have it. In fact, I hope you would give it to your first born son. It might save his life one day. Now I must be going. I have a taxi waiting outside to take me back to Mayo. Just then Grace's mom Alannah entered the pub from the kitchen and walked over to Porter. They both had tears in their eyes as they hugged. Porter said, "Alannah, we have both lost a very caring and lovely man in Callahan. He was a friend to me years ago in America when I had no friends and was lost. He knew exactly what to say and picked the right time to say it. He will be missed by all who knew him, a real gentleman. I learned from him that you don't need an education to be a gentleman, but you need a supportive spouse like you to be a good parent. As I watched and listened to your children, I could see that you must have been a wonderful mother to them. They were discussing ways they were going to care for you as

you get older. I wish I had a family like yours to care for me."
Grace then came from behind the counter and put her arms
around Alannah to say, "Mom, you raised a wonderful family,
and we will all be here for you. We can't replace Callahan, but
we will be the next best." She asked Porter to come visit again
sometime, and said she would walk with him to visit Callahan in
the graveyard.

Callahan's oldest son now took over the pub. The
following year Grace had another son whom they christened
Ryan. Three daughters followed him. Shannon became very
attached to Grace and Richard's sons as the years passed. As the
children arrived, Richard and Grace moved several times to
larger accommodations. He gave up butchering, and became a
very successful businessman. He also became an alcoholic.
Grace kept pointing out how lucky she was to have married him
and how happy she was. In return, Richard would tell Grace, "If
it were not for you, I have no idea where I might have ended up.
You have made me a very happy man." When she answered, "I
think we could be much happier if you give up the drink," he
knew she was right. She stood by him as he struggled to quit,
and finally he did. He would do anything for her.

Chapter 18

Shannon Leaves Home

Shannon eventually left home, never knowing she was the skeleton in the closest, and went to work for a record company in England. She met and married a very good-looking man named Martin. They had no children. As the years went on most of the Richard and Grace's family left home, some traveling as far as the United States. When their second son Ryan went to New York, he regularly stayed in touch with most of the family. Like all his siblings he respected his dad, and returned home when his dad died. In fact, they thought he was the best dad anyone could have. It was on this trip home that his mother told him about her daughter Shannon. The secret she carried all her life had hurt Grace tremendously. She explained why Shannon was raised as her sister, telling Ryan that it was Callahan and Alannah's way of allowing her to have a happily married life with someone. Grace asked Ryan to sit down with her, so she could tell him how she had suffered for so many years by not being able to share her secret with Shannon. "Your father and I had a very happy life together, and we loved and cared for each other. We often talked about Shannon and how the priest told us when Shannon was born that we were to let her be raised as my sister by Callahan and Alannah, otherwise I would have no life. There were days and nights I have cried and wondered if the priest was right.

"I wanted so many times to tell Shannon who she was, but the fear of her running away to hide was all I could bear. I spoke with your dad many times wondering if we should tell you and your siblings, but your father always said as long as he was alive the it would not be shared. Now that he is dead, I feel I should share the secret so it does not die with me. But my sharing it now with Shannon will destroy her life. I'm sure her husband would not be as understanding as your father was. He might just take off and leave her. Ryan, I have had a great life with your father but something was missing, I needed to share it with somebody, and God seemed to be telling me that you are the person best suited in as much as you and Shannon have always been so close.

"Let me share this with you. When I found out I was pregnant with Shannon, I spent days wandering around the fields, and a lot of time by the waterfall. I don't think I wanted to drown myself, but I was not myself. I kept beating myself up and asking myself how I could let this happen but then again, because of the times I was not told anything about sex. All the kids learned about sex by watching the bull mount the cow and or the dogs, as we used to say, getting connected in the yard. My mother would always say to us as we left the house, 'Be careful and stay out of trouble.' We thought it was that we should not raid someone's apple orchard or throw a stone through the neighbor's window. Shannon's father, she never mentioned his name, would come into the pub for a drink and I only dated him twice. When this happened, we were both young and never thought anything about the outcome. Then he started to date another girl from the next village when I started to get sick, which I now know was morning sickness I would go into the cowshed. I was telling a neighbor that I did not feel well, and she knew right away what was wrong. She asked if she would go with me when I told my parents. I said, 'No, they will send me away.' I spent days crying and walking the fields. Then one day I was really worried, and I headed down to the waterfall, and as I was sitting with my feet in the water, my dad arrived and I told him. My mom and dad were the only friends I had. Imagine if I were put away into a home and the baby sold to someone as we often heard when we listen in on people whispering about someone. My dad and mom were really great people, and somehow they came up with the idea that they would raise the baby as my sister rather than put me into a mothers' baby home which was run by the nuns.

"When Shannon was born, we took her to be baptized and the priest asked where the father was because he would need to sign the papers.

My dad told him who he was but that he was a creep, and I would be better off not having him in my life. So, the priest filled the baptismal certificate 'father not known,' and that automatically classed Shannon as a bastard child. The next day the priest paid a visit to Shannon's father and told him he must marry the girl. That's when he conned Callahan into putting his mark on the paper, so he could get a passport for America. I found out afterwards that Callahan was only too happy to sign so he would get him as far away from me as possible. My dad knew better than I did. Shannon's father was a no-good bastard. But I was in love with him that's what's made the hurt worse. And after he left for America, I was still hoping he would send for me and Shannon.

"No one knows where he ended up in America. Ryan, I was young, and without anyone knowing it I applied for a passport and booked my passage on a ship to Boston. I was in love with the bastard. Now that Shannon was taken care of, I was going to find her father, but at the last minute, I canceled and did not board the ship for Boston. What people will do when they are young and in love! For the next few years I did not know what was going to happen to me. Then your father came into the pub and my life was changed overnight, I knew I could have a life with this man. Ryan, I ask you to promise me you will not reveal what I told you to anyone, as long as I am alive. I know after I'm dead you will handle it right. You are the best one to tell Shannon who she really is."

Three years later, Ryan received a telegram from Western Union telling him that his mother Grace only had a few days to live. Ryan was hoping to get there before she died, but he was late by a few hours. Her death unnerved him completely. All the family was there for the funeral. Shannon came home from England with her husband Martin. The mourners cried openly in the cemetery. The priest thanked everyone for traveling from afar. He said the family would like to invite all who wanted to join them at the hotel for food and drinks in a few hours. After the priest said the prayers and left, most of the people went to visit other grave sites of their relatives who were buried in the same cemetery. Ryan and Shannon along with her husband Martin were the last ones to leave. Martin said, "I will walk ahead and you two can catch up on old times. You have not seen one another for some time."

That gave Ryan the opening he needed to talk to Shannon. Ryan and Shannon cried some more and hugged one another. Shannon said, "I'm so sorry you did not get here to see your mom before she died." Ryan replied, "But you were here?" She answered, "Yes. I was sitting on the side of her bed, and just before she closed her eyes and died, she almost broke my fingers as she held my hand. It was as if she wanted to tell me something. She would ease up and then squeeze my hand again. Whatever she was trying to tell me I guess I will never know." Ryan said, "Yes, you will know, and I will tell you right now because I know what she wanted to tell you." "You do?" "Yes, she asked me to tell you after she was dead. Please sit down here on this rock, and I will tell you." Ryan began by holding her hands, and then he continued, "You and I are very close." Shannon nodded, "Yes, we always have been." "Well, what she wanted me to tell you is that, you and I are brother and sister. Grace was not your sister but your mother." They cried together, and Shannon asked, "Who else knows about this? Do your brother and sisters?" "Not yet. I will tell them after you return to England." Shannon and Martin could not come into the hotel because they were taking the next bus to the ferry to return to England. Shannon whispered, "Please do not say anything to my husband about this right now, but call me in a few days."

Ryan rented a room in town so as not to burden anyone. After the burial and before leaving to return to New York, he sat down with his siblings and shared the secret with them. He had no idea how they really felt about finding a long-lost sister. He saw, however, that his brother Connor was excited on hearing the news. Afterward, Connor would refer to her as his sister, he would send her birthday cards, which read "from a brother to a sister." Shannon told Ryan she liked receiving the cards, but would not elaborate anymore.

Ryan and Shannon were always very close, and that was probably the reason why Grace picked him to tell Shannon who she really was. After Ryan returned to New York, he and Shannon chatted many times over the phone. Ryan asked if she ever thought of taking a trip to New York. "Funny you should ask. I have often wanted to go to America and visit all the places where my father was when he was there. He used to tell me stories about a place called Pittsburg where he worked. He would talk about his friend Porter and Duff Murphy who got him a job working in the mines.

"Callahan and Alannah have been the best parents to me, caring for me and never cross with me. Now that I have spent so many days crying since you told me who I really am, I think I am ready to talk and listen to you. Tell me this, 'When did you come to know that I was your sister?'" Ryan explained, "When my dad died, our mother filled me in on her younger days, how your father had run away and left her to fend for you and herself." Shannon retorted, "I wish you would not refer to her as my 'mother.' She was not a mother to me. Callahan and

Alannah were my mom and dad. However, I will tell you this ever since you told me at the cemetery who I was, it has changed my life. I cannot get a good night's sleep. My mind keeps drifting back to my childhood and all the names I was called from the kids when I was going to school and the finger-pointing and I never knew what those kids probably knew. They probably heard it from their parents who used my mother as an example in teaching them how to stay out of trouble. I am so happy to be here in England, and not worry about meeting people who might have known about me years ago."

Every time Ryan called her, he could tell she wanted to dig deeper into her mother's life as a child. It was months before she started to ask any questions about her who her father might be. When Ryan told her that he went to America after she was born, that seemed to open up another can of worms with her. She said, "You are in America. Can you find out where he might have lived? Do you think the bastard might be dead. I should not say that; after all, he is my father even if he may not want to admit it. But if I ever find him, I will spit on his face, and then I will call him a bastard. Do you think I might have any brothers or sisters? Could I get some information through the back door so as not to disgrace her by asking someone who might tell someone who would get it back to her friends in England. I don't want to be known as a bastard child. That is as low as you can go."

Ryan did his best to bring her self-esteem up a little by telling her that she was loved by everyone. She seemed happier before he told her who she was, and now he was feeling guilty. He kept telling himself he should never have told her. Her biggest fear was that her husband would find out. She also had a best friend, an Irish woman whom she had known ever since she went to England. Even though they were very close, she never told her. Ryan would chat with her twice a week from New York, and as time went on she became very forgiving. One time she told Ryan she could not forgive Grace for not telling her. Ryan decided to take a trip to England and stay with her for a few days, so they could catch up on the past. It was a trip well worth taking to see the joy in her face when Ryan entered her apartment. At the time, Ryan was hoping she would and could forgive all the people from her past who caused her hurt.

She held Ryan's hands before asking him to sit down. Then she started talking about her past and what she was remembering. "I remembered all those kids and how mean they were to me when I was going to school. And they knew what I did not know. I had many a fight in school defending my sister. I could have been told who I was at the time. I never went home and told anyone how I was treated, how my dress was ripped by one of the boys and how they made me remove my shoes and walk barefooted on thistles they put on the road. I was often called a bastard. However, I always defended my name. Now I know what I did not know then, that they were right. They called me by my right name that was the name of my father. But I did not know at the time. Since you told me his name and where he was from, I am sure I had many a fight with his family members at the time. On my God, come on and sit down I never stop talking. Ryan, I am so happy you came to visit me. I always knew we were close. I always knew you were special, and I can see now why your mother picked you as the go-between in helping to set me straight. I remember one time a kid called Grace a whore. I never knew I was the offspring of all that until you told me.

"Ryan, how long are you staying? Let me show you around. I am so excited you are here. Give me another hug, brother.

How is our brother back in Ireland?" That's the first time Ryan ever heard her closing the gap in the family. It was if she was doing her best to make up for lost time and to become part of this new found family she had missed out on all those years. Ryan was so happy now he could swallow the words that he had thought of, like he was sorry he told her who she was. Ryan said he was only staying one night and he was going to Ireland to visit his brother. He hesitated and repeated himself; "I mean 'our brother'," and was staying there one night before returning to New York. Ryan, Grace, and Martin went out to dinner that evening. They all chatted but avoided talking about the family in Ireland. Shannon had asked Ryan not to tell Martin under any circumstances. They all had a few drinks, and on the way home they stopped to introduce Ryan to her Irish girlfriend. Again Shannon warned Ryan not to say anything to her because Ryan's wife came from the next town to her in Ireland. At this point Ryan appreciated the quote from Walter Scott, "O, what a tangled web we weave when first we practice to deceive".

Before Ryan left the next morning, Shannon asked him to call her from New York to answer the additional questions she will have. Then she gave him a big hug, one of those hugs she was missing all her life. Ryan took the ferry to Dublin and then a train to Galway to meet with his brother who was just as excited as Shannon was when she met Ryan. They spent hours talking about Shannon and rehashing the family history. They pointed out how the secrets were not really secrets at all since they were there under everyone's noses. The last person to know the secret is the person it's all about. The two brothers who were very close growing up enjoyed their time together. They had dinner at the same hotel they ate in after the mother was buried, they visited the grave, and Ryan headed home to New York the next day.

A few weeks went by before he called Shannon, they chatted, and he could tell that his visit gave her the boost she really needed. Shannon said, "Now to my questions. Is there any way you can find out if I might have any siblings, and could my father be still alive? Where in America did my father go?" Ryan agreed to do some research for her and let her know the outcome. Shannon didn't want to die until she found out. Ryan told her he would do his best, but she should not be too disappointed. If her father were as shrewd as they say he was, he would have left no trails to follow. From time to time, she would change the subject. She told Ryan that one time as a child someone called her by a different last name, and she quickly reprimanded him that that was not her name since her last name was the same as Alannah's. Shannon was ever so happy that now someone had told her who she was. She did say she knew growing up that something was different, but until now, she could not put her finger on it. She said, "I find myself like a fish out of the water. You are the only one I have now. Callahan, Alannah, Francis, Griffin, Brady, Richard, Grace, they are all dead. It's as though I have lost everything in my past life." Ryan could tell she was still hurting, and would hurt until the day she died. Ryan never got any reaction from most of his siblings concerning whether they were pleased or not about finding a long-lost sister, except for his brother Connor who also kept in touch with Shannon by phone or mail.

Ryan started his research after he returned to the states, contacting some friends and asking them to check out certain things, but to keep it under their hats. Shannon had asked Ryan to do his best in finding out the answers, but not to ask too many questions. Ryan was thinking she must be going through hell looking back on her life, and never having received a hug from her mother. One-time Ryan was chatting with her on the phone when he mentioned "our mother". Shannon must have been having a bad day because she was quick to tell him, "She was not our mother. She was your mother not mine. She was not there for me. It was your grandmother who was really my mother when I was sick, when I made my communion, my confirmation. So, please don't call her our mother."

Chapter 19

Shannon Dies

A year later, Ryan received a phone call from England
telling him that Shannon had died. Ryan called his brother in
Ireland with the news, and they agreed to meet at London's
airport. Shannon's friend Jim, who had made the call to Ryan,
was there to meet them, and explained that Shannon called him a
few days earlier telling him she did not feel well. When he
visited her, she asked that if something should happen to her,
would he call Ryan in New York right away and left the phone
number. Ryan inquired, "Jim, how did you come to know
Shannon?" "Oh, I am a cousin of her late husband. She was such
a beautiful lady who stayed inside her little circle that not too
many people were invited to enter. She always talked about
Ryan her cousin who lived in New York. She thought the world
of you. Whenever we went out to dinner, your name always
came up, and she would say, 'I was just talking with my cousin
Ryan in New York.' She said she has another cousin in Galway,
Ryan's brother Bob, and he would send her cards on Christmas

and birthdays and that. Ryan, she was lost after her husband died. I think I met you that time. You only stayed a day or so. I was working up north at the time, but I came down to Martin's funeral and had to leave right after. Shannon told me that you and Connor are first or second cousins." "Well, Jim, now that she has passed away, I can tell you who we really are. The cousins Shannon told you about were her brothers." "What? You mean she was your sister?" "Yes, Jim, she was my sister." "Oh boy, that's news! No wonder she was always changing her stories, even to her husband. It was as if she were living a lie. Did she really know who she was? I remember at times how fast she would change the subject even when she and her husband were talking. It must be a hard way to live."

I will drop you at the undertakers, and I'm sure you are hungry. There is a fine restaurant across the street from the undertakers where I could meet you later this evening. Ryan and Connor went to the undertakers for a viewing, and it was so sad. Ryan wanted to just lift Shannon up and give her a big hug. Instead, he just whispered in her ear, "Don't be mad at my mother when you see her; she will be there with open arms waiting for you. That is not a place where they spread gossip;

everyone is equal." Not too many family members came for the burial, but some cousins did come from Galway. That's when Ryan told them that Shannon was his sister. They were stunned. They always thought she was their aunt, when, instead, she was their first cousin. After the burial, all were invited for food and drinks to Shannon's Irish friend's house. She was also stunned on finding out Shannon had brothers and sisters. She told Ryan that in all the years she knew her, she never said anything. That was Shannon. She died as she had lived, a stranger to herself and a stranger to all the people who knew her.

THE END